The Berlin Escape

Victor O. Swatsek

8/2017

Hi Kathy & Erich.

Please enjoy

Victor O. Swatsek
VOS & Associates
Palm Desert, CA
www.NovelsByVic.com
victorswatsek@aol.com

Library of Congress _____
© 2017 by Victor O. Swatsek

First published by VOS & Associates

ISBN 10: 154892220X
ISBN 13: 9781548922207

Printed in the United States

This book is printed on acid free paper

Because of the dynamic nature of the Internet, any web addresses or links contained in this book may have been changed since publication and may no longer be valid. The views expressed in this work are solely those of the author.

I dedicate this book to my wife, Elizabeth, who is also my closest friend. She has been my inspiration from the very beginning of my writing career.

I would also like to thank my family and close friends, who have become my first line editors, and have encouraged me to continue this challenging and satisfying journey.
I also, want to thank my muses, Prince Alexander, and Prince Blueberry and now my new "muse", Cinnamon.

PROLOGUE

"Why are people trying to kill me?' Walter asked Duncan.

"My guess is that it's because you're rich," Duncan said looking at him. "And that means you're an easy target."

"While that may be true, Duncan, we need to find this Apollo and fast," Walter said. "And find out who and why someone put a contract out to kill me. In addition, Rick just informed me that two other French women were seen checking out the Monarch Ranch. All of them seemed to be well informed – perhaps too well informed."

"This is the second major attempt on your life since I met you," Duncan said. "Is it possible it's a jealous competitor?"

"No, I'm afraid not," Walter said. "I think it's closer to home."

❖　❖　❖

Duncan was driving Walter to the New York Botanical Gardens where he often wen, to enjoy the serenity and get away from his business world. While driving, he received a phone call.

"Hello?" asked Walter.

"Walter, this is General Howard Metcaff."

"Well hello, Howard," Walter said, surprised by the call. "How are you and the family doing?"

"They're fine Walter," he said, as he was hurriedly driving.

"What can I do for you?" asked Walter.

"Walter, I think I'm in deep trouble," said the General, sounding nervous. "You said if I ever needed help, to call on you. Well, I'm making that call now!"

"General you seem deeply worried," Walter said. "How about we meet somewhere and talk about it?"

"That would be great," said the General sounding somewhat relieved. "How about today at the *French Onion* restaurant on 5th Avenue in downtown New York?"

"Splendid, Howard," he said. "I know exactly where that is. I'll see you in about thirty minutes," and he hung up.

Walter didn't like the sound in Howard's voice. *Something must really terrify him to call me,* he thought.

"Duncan...take us to the *French Onion* restaurant on 5th Avenue," Walter said.

"Yes Mr. Donleavy," Duncan said.

As they were getting closer to the restaurant, Walter could hear a fire engine, an emergency ambulance and police sirens in the distance.

❖   ❖   ❖

A special ceremonial crown was created and given to an Egyptian woman named Nephritides in the year 14 B.C. It was made of solid gold, encrusted with diamonds, rubies and emeralds. Very few people had ever seen it. However, there had been rumors about its existence ever since an unusually small and nondescript pyramid was discovered on the outskirts of Luxor, Egypt. In 1934, the pyramid was found close to the Gulf of Suez, hidden by sand dunes that had engulfed it completely by many sand storms, over the course of almost two thousand years. The workers labored for over a year, moving sand and rock in the hope of finding the lost pyramid. Once the sands were sufficiently removed, they saw a unique door. Hieroglyphics were cut deep into the red limestone rock of the entrance of the pyramid.

The hieroglyphics on the outer wall told the story of a special jewel-laden gold crown Nephritides received from the reigning Pharaoh. However, when the tomb was opened in 1934 by the famous Egyptologist, Sir Hillary von Peterborough, the crown of jewels was not in sight. Nothing of value was found, so they abandoned the pyramid. It was thought that the markings on the outside were a ruse to thwart grave robbers. This was the first time the tomb had been opened – or so they thought. Even more mysterious were the special seals that were not broken which would insure its security.

If the crown were ever found, the purported value in 1934 would have been in the millions. In today's market – it would be priceless. It was a mystery, until the story surfaced around early 1945, when the papyrus scrolls appeared again, and supposedly identified the location of the pyramid.

❖   ❖   ❖

An individual in Paris was known as Apollinaris Bonnaire, but her inner circle called her Apollo. However, what most people didn't know was that she led one of the largest criminal organizations in Europe. She lived on the outskirts of Paris in a palace she called *Chateau de Carlson*. This was her haven, and her headquarters to conduct her business. Very few people were ever allowed into her inner sanctum. Only women guarded her. They were proficient in various self-defense and assassination techniques. In her world, she was almost invisible. All her associates were single, with no family to distract them from their training and their work.

They were recruited from all kinds of lifestyles, with one purpose – to guard Apollo and do her bidding, which was to assassinate individuals. The job paid very well. The gun of choice for all her operatives to use was a custom-built, small-caliber pistol with a special built-in silencer. It also included a special "thumb" print recognition unique to the person to whom it was assigned. They were trained as highly skilled operatives, using a variety of weapons. Each was also taught how to be womanly and desirable to men. They were also taught how to dress for every occasion, wear the right jewelry, and, of course how to converse.

Chapter

1

It was October of 1946. Walter had just jumped through a window of the private train of Colonel Alexander Baryshnikov, the Russian Colonel who had liberated the inmates at Sachsenhausen Concentration Camp. As Walter jumped off the train, he rolled over several times in the high shrubs and stayed there for what felt like an inordinate amount of time to make sure it was safe to get up. He caught his breath and finally got up to begin his long trek. He went in the opposite direction and through the forests, staying off the main roads. Several days later, one very cold and damp night as he was camped beside Lake Schwielowsee, he heard voices in the distance, which broadcasted like an echo chamber. He quickly put out his small fire and froze in place.

"He must be here somewhere," a guard called out, seeming to be in a semi-drunk stupor. "The Colonel gave us specific orders not to come back without him."

I have to get out of here, Walter thought. He got up, and started to slowly back away, until he was almost to the edge of the lake. He hid behind a large oak tree, hoping it was enough to shield him. This time of year, the leaves fell silently, like a whisper to the ground. However, when he walked on them, the dried leaves crunched under his feet and almost gave away his hiding place. He could tell there were two of them, because he saw two flash-lights bobbing through the dense and dark forest. Both appeared to be somewhat drunk, stumbling and bumping against trees.

They walked towards Walter, without knowing he was hiding behind a large tree. Walter tried not to panic. He didn't know where to run, so he stayed hidden, hoping they would give up. They got within fifteen feet of him, and all the while Walter prayed for a miracle.

Suddenly Walter woke up in a cold sweat in his bed. *My God, I keep having these reoccurring dreams of that particular night*, he thought. He lay back down on his bed and thought, *Thank heavens it was only a dream.* He got up, took a shower and just sat on the stool in his bathroom for what seemed like an hour, when it was actually only minutes. It was 1992, and he looked around his opulent bathroom, with light green, variegated onyx counter tops. He remembered when he had made all the special modifications. He installed a *panic room* behind what looked like a regular door to one of his many closets. In twenty-some-odd years – he had never used it. Another *panic room* only much larger was installed in his library. *Why am I thinking of this,* he wondered. *I guess that's the reason they call it a panic room.*

This particular morning he took longer getting dressed before going downstairs to meet with Hilda, his housekeeper, and have breakfast. Walter always dressed as if he was going to an office downtown, when in fact he just went to his library. He typically wore a blue pinstriped, double-breasted suit with a dark blue necktie. Hilda started preparing his breakfast in the kitchen as soon as she heard Walter's footsteps on the stairs.

"Good morning Mr. Donleavy," said Hilda, smiling as always.

"Good morning Hilda," he replied.

"What would you like for breakfast this morning?" she asked.

"I think I'll just have my usual," he said, continuing to glance through the newspaper as he sat down at the table.

After he had his breakfast, he walked into his library to listen to the latest stock market reports on his TV and read the morning reports about his companies. However, this particular morning, he didn't have the enthusiasm he normally had. He turned to a channel on his television and listened to the news. One item particularly perked his interest. They talked about a robbery at the Sir William Sheffield Museum in London, England. He knew it well, because before the war, when he was an assistant as a bank clerk at the Bank of England, he would spend almost all of his free time studying the old masters, like Rembrandt, Van Gogh, Matisse, Raphael and Goya. He received his inspiration to paint from those masters at that museum.

❖ ❖ ❖

Walter Donleavy had a dark past that he didn't want many people to know about, except a very select few. Towards the end of the Second World War, he was interned at Sachsenhausen

Concentration Camp located just outside of Berlin, Germany. His real name was Alfred Berger, and he possessed a unique skill that enabled him to survive some of the cruelties of war. He was handpicked to become the chief engraver for creating the counterfeit English Banknotes that were printed at the camp. Hitler was going to use this counterfeit money, mostly to pay for needed equipment and armaments to fight the war, but also to distribute, for the purpose of destroying the English economy.

Walter also had another unique skill – he was a painter who had mastered the technique to create counterfeit oil paintings. One such individual remembered his skill, because he had painted a portrait of him, which was hanging in his bank in Bayern, Germany.

❖   ❖   ❖

He traveled from Berlin to Florence, and then on to Marseille, where he was able to book passage on a cargo ship bound for New Orleans. He created a new passport and paperwork for himself and changed his name to Walter Donleavy. He ultimately settled in Providence, Rhode Island. He had a small apartment he stayed in at first. At the time, it took care of all of his needs. He didn't socialize with anybody, which left him free to spend time watching and learning about the various markets.

His first venture was buying a small company that sold limited edition prints and some inexpensive oil paintings at discount prices. After about two years, he opened around three hundred stores in the United States by selling franchises, and after four years, went public and made a small fortune. He purchased other companies and typically sold off some of the assets, turned the companies around to be profitable, and then resold some of them at a handsome profit. Some of the companies he kept, because they complimented his other business interests.

Along the way, he recruited several people to assist him to reach his goals. That included personal security for himself, information specialists and an individual who was actually the face of Monarch Enterprises.

❖ ❖ ❖

He made his fortune by purchasing various small companies, which he felt, had great potential, because they were in either trouble or were mismanaged. Over the years, Walter had acquired various businesses, with a long-term goal of being able to operate his companies from anywhere in the world. It wasn't to become a recluse, but at the time, he wanted to stay in the background and not be very visible.

Chapter

2

Sachsenhausen Concentration camp was situated just outside of Berlin, Germany. There was a special section built just for inmates that knew anything about the printing and counterfeiting industry. They were not allowed to converse with other people at the camp.

The camp commandant asked everyone about his or her abilities in that area. Walter said yes, in anticipation that if I said no, he might be dead that day. They were looking for an individual who could assemble a staff with various printing expertise to perform high level printing functions and wanted Walter in charge of quality control for the product. He said he had some printing experience and I knew of some people who could help.

The Colonel said, "We want to create counterfeit five, ten, twenty and fifty pound English banknotes."

Walter asked him, "How many?"

The Colonel said, "Around fifteen million to start and possibly more as time goes on."

Walter gave him a list, besides the ones that were already with here and told him these were who he knew would like to have as part of the group, plus various supplies and equipment. He said he would make this his priority and would see me in a week.

Two days later, after having identified the people, they were loaded onto trucks and driven to the new location.

They arrived after an eight-hour ride in a drafty old truck. After they disembarked from the truck, they were immediately introduced to the current group that was already creating counterfeit documents – specifically passports and birth certificates. The new people were afraid until they walked into the barracks, which had single beds with blankets and fresh clothes and a bathroom with a hot shower. At one point, there were over one hundred forty prisoners from ten different countries working in this enormous counterfeiting ring. Their only concern, like the others, was what would happen after they completed these tasks. They were assured that for the time being, at least they got better treatment than the other prisoners did.

Some countries must have known they just didn't know where it was being done. Suddenly the German mark was worthless and most supplies were paid using English banknotes. England at the time were very pro Germany and the Duke of Windsor liked Hitler. Back in the camp, some felt guilty that we were treated better, because at night, they could hear screams, and some were even shot. There was always dissension of some type going on in the group because they knew Hitler was running out of money and the more money that was printed the longer the war was going to continue.

Hitler's plan was named *Operation Bernhart*, and he was going to destroy the English economy, plus help pay for some of the cost of the war. They almost succeeded and one point the camp was instructed to create plates for the US one-hundred dollar bill. It proved to be more difficult because it was printed on both sides and you needed an entirely different printing press.

Chapter

3

The crown rumor surfaced again in 1941 when German General Jürgen Fieldmeister was patrolling northern Africa. One evening he was having dinner with Dr. Benjamin Fazihd, the head curator of a small Egyptian museum named The Heliopolis Museum. He was also the assistant curator of the world famous Sir William Sheffield Museum in London, England.

"General Fieldmeister," said Dr. Fazihd. "Have you ever heard of the crown of Nephritides?"

"No I have not," said the General. "However, I have a feeling you're going to tell me." He sat back and enjoyed one of his special cigars and his Napoléon Mandarin liqueur in a Baccarat crystal snifter.

Dr. Fazihd went into detail of how Princess Nephritides, while not an actual queen, was given all the rights and privileges of a queen, by the then reigning Pharaoh King Sekhemkhet.

"Why are you telling me this story?" asked the General. "I have no interest in something that I'm told is a fable. You said there was a map of sorts, showing the location. But did they ever find any type of entrance?"

"Not recently. But that's because there was a secret second entrance that King Sekhemkhet had added that very few people knew about," Dr. Fazihd said.

"How could that be possible?" asked the General, who was suddenly more attentive, sitting up and keen to know more.

"In order to build the *special* second entrance," said Dr. Fazihd, "the Pharaoh had to have a drawing specially created that revealed the location of the pyramid, and the second door."

"But by now those drawings can't still be around, can they?" inquired the General.

"Actually they are," said Dr. Fazihd sounding jubilant. "And I have them."

"What? Are you serious?" exclaimed the General. *He can't be serious after all this time.* He thought. "How could you have gotten them?"

"Remember, I am also the assistant head curator at the Sir William Sheffield Museum in London," said Dr. Fazihd. "They appeared one day mixed in with another batch of old papyrus scrolls. The reason it didn't set off any alarms, was that it was written in a dialect very few people can read and understand today. In other words, it was like reading the ancient Egyptian language, but in a *slang* version."

"So....again I ask. Why are you telling me this?" asked the General.

"I will tell you," said Dr. Fazihd. "But first, I must ask you to be very discreet about what I am about to tell you."

"Agreed," said the General, who was not in the habit of being spoon-fed information that may or may-not be authentic, much less valuable.

"As you know, Adolf Hitler believed in the occult," said Dr. Fazihd. "It is my understanding that he was is in possession of a document, which could give us the exact location of the pyramid and would show us the exact location of the special door to the pyramid. The people that originally discovered what they thought was the pyramid had all died and information was lost over time. Once we locate the pyramid with *his* document, then with *my* document, we can find where the second secret door is that holds the special crown."

"What kind of nonsense is this," said the frustrated General. "I have been with Hitler many times, and he has never mentioned or even hinted of any such document."

"While that may be true," said Dr. Fazihd, "Nonetheless, as I'm sure you know, it has been rumored that Hitler is somewhat paranoid. He may just wish to keep this to himself and his special inner-circle of friends. After all, the crown's value is considered priceless."

I may have to give this more serious consideration, he thought. The General stood up casually and brushed his rather large bushy grey mustache from side to side as if it needed to be combed.

"This is such a preposterous story…..that it might just be true," said the General adjusting his monocle.

"I assure you that all that I have just told you….is true," said Dr. Fazihd. "My question to you is this. Are you interested in a share of the treasure…..that is so unique, that your name will be written in the history books?"

The General didn't give him an answer, but said, "How do you propose we obtain these plans from Hitler?"

"Firstly *you* must visit with Hitler at his home in Berchtesgaden," said Dr. Fazihd. "Try to get a one-on-one visit with him. Talk a little about the occult and slowly talk about the crown. Don't give him too much information and allow him to make comments. Maybe he'll even disclose where he has the document."

"What will you be doing while I visit with Hitler?" asked the General.

"I'm going to fly to London to retrieve *my* documents," said Dr. Fazihd, ecstatic. Now that he had an ally.

"It will be difficult to visit with Hitler, because he is always traveling," said the General. "When will I see you again?"

"I should be back within the week," said Dr. Fazihd. "In the meantime, see if you can get those scrolls from Hitler."

❖   ❖   ❖

The General left Dr. Fazihd's office, grumbling, trying to figure out how he was going to see Hitler. As he walked back to his hotel, he passed several lively bars and decided he was going in to have some fun. As he stood in the doorway, he surveyed the room to see if he recognized anyone. Not seeing anybody he knew, he went in and sat at a table, waiting for the server to come over.

"Do you have any Napoléon Mandarin liqueur," the General asked.

"Why of course we do sir," he said. "I'll be right back."

Chapter

4

Walter had invited Rick and Liz to his estate in Providence, Rhode Island. He also asked them to bring Frank Richter, the CFO for the Monarch Ranch with them. Leonard Schultz was going to be in town that week with a specific plan he had developed with Walter to realign all of Walter's business interests. This would also give Frank some insight into Walter's business dealings, which included the new companies both Rick and Liz, would be responsible to manage.

"I'm looking forward to spending some time with Leonard Schultz, since he was so involved in Mr. Donleavy's business," said Frank happy to be invited.

"This meeting is going to be about breaking up Walter's business interests," Rick said. "At the end, we will have three corporations. Walter will retain the companies he still wants to control and Liz and I will manage the rest of them."

"This also sounds like I'll need to hire more people to manage all of these companies if we're going to keep all of this going in the right direction," Frank said.

"Hey wait a minute," Liz said chiming in. "I think I should have my own CFO to handle my own business interests."

"I would agree," Rick said coyly. "Walter has a main office, even though he doesn't reside there, with a staff that has managed his businesses and was overseen by Leonard Schultz, his then COO and CFO. We might want to see if any of them would like to transfer and move to Fort Collins. This way we don't have to hire and train new people."

"Yeah, I agree, that makes good sense," Liz said happily.

Rick looked at Liz and just grinned. *She's come a long way,* he thought, *from her days of teaching and giving lectures at the Universities on languages around the world.*

"On our way over, we should stop in Billings and see how Dwight is doing with the new meat processing plant," Rick said. "We can easily do that before we fly on to Walter's meeting at his house in Providence."

❖ ❖ ❖

In the previous week, in another part of Europe, a meeting had taken place with an individual that had taken out a contract and had vowed to kill Walter Donleavy.

"Are you sure you can get the job done?" he asked. "I've outlined how and when I want it done and in a specific sequence and time frame. Once I leave here, the only time I want you to contact me, is when you have completed your task!"

"Please do not worry," Ulrich said. "I have an individual and she has never failed me before, and we don't intend to start now."

"Do not get too cocky!" he shouted. "He has people at his beck and call night and day."

"Again, do not worry," they repeated, trying to reassure his client. "We will prepare by researching him and his friends, and then create a plan that my people will follow to the letter."

"I'm also paying you a lot of money," he said. "Do not fail me. I have no tolerance for failure!" and hung up the phone.

Ulrich said on the phone, "Well you heard him, we cannot fail. If we fail, it will not only hurt us financially, but it could potentially ruin me."

Chapter

5

Richard Teaubel had his name changed to Rick Benedict, after he came over from West Germany in 1955. He was only five years old and stayed with his uncle, Walter Donleavy. Since Rick didn't speak a word of English, Walter hired a special tutor to teach him the language. Four months later, still with a slight accent, he was enrolled at Mount St. Albans, a prominent military prep school in Providence, Rhode Island.

When he graduated, he went on to St. Basil's, which was also a private school in Providence. He received his Bachelor's in history and completed his Master's in art and architectural history from Columbia University, majoring in the historical European era. He received his second Master's in Mechanical Engineering also from Columbia. At the time, he was considering being a high-rise building engineer. Rick knew he liked teaching and several excellent universities had courted him.

After a year of teaching, Rick got a notice in the mail from *Uncle Sam* that said he was drafted into the Army. Since he had degrees in several subjects, they recommended that he apply to Officer Candidate School (OCS). After a battery of tests during OCS training at Fort Bliss, Texas, the Army felt he had a higher calling and gave him orders for Advanced Infantry Training (AIT) at Fort Belvoir in West Virginia. After completing the training, he was promoted to Second Lieutenant.

Rick's Military Occupational Specialty (MOS) was a Nike Hercules Missile Maintenance Repair Platoon Leader. He received his promotion to First Lieutenant as soon as he completed that part of his training. Two weeks later, he shipped out to Zweibrucken, West Germany. When he got there, he was reassigned, and his final assignment was as a cipher code expert, supervising ten other individuals. After ten months in his new position, he was promoted to the rank of Captain and head of the department. However, after two years, that quickly grew boring and not challenging enough. He wanted to do something more exciting and fulfilling. As he finished his tour of duty, he was asked repeatedly to re-enlist, but each time he declined.

"I want to get back to teaching, Sir," Rick said to the Major Recruiting Officer.

❖ ❖ ❖

Rick was handsome, with a chiseled jaw, blond hair, and blue eyes. He left the service, went back to school and became a professor at Brown University. Over the past four to five years, he'd taken a break from teaching and helped Walter with some of his problems related to some new businesses he purchased. It also became financially rewarding for Walter as well as for Rick.

Using the skills he learned in the service, he turned a ranch that was used to entertain clients, into a working cattle ranch. They renamed it – Monarch Ranch

❖ ❖ ❖

Walter also purchased the *Balducci Couture* firm located in Tel Aviv, Israel. He converted the company from producing cloth for the fashion industry, into making the finest Persian-like rugs. To support that business, they also purchased two llama and alpaca ranches. One in Carrizozo, New Mexico and the other in San Ignacio, Bolivia. Rick managed the two ranches that supplied all the wool for the *Balducci Couture*.

❖ ❖ ❖

Elizabeth Bowen, who changed her name to Elizabeth Hildebrand, came to Providence, Rhode Island, in 1956 when she was five years old. She was an immigrant from Linz, Austria, when her parents shipped her to the United States to live with her Uncle Walter and to get an education. She was enrolled in Sister of Passionate Sorrow, an exclusive school for girls in upper New York. She studied the English language from a very early age.

She graduated with honors and had offers from the ten top Ivy League universities. She settled on Radcliffe University, because they had the best classes for her long-term goals. She graduated from Radcliffe, with a Bachelor's degree in political science. Liz went on to Columbia University for her Master's and PhD in languages. By the time she graduated, she was proficient in six foreign languages. She had an offer to work at the U.N. as a multiple language translator, but declined.

Upon graduation, her Uncle Walter drove her down to the Conanicut Harbor in Jamestown Rhode Island. He presented her with a Ferretti 74 yacht, complete with a full-time captain. She was overwhelmed by a present like this.

"Oh my," exclaimed Liz. "This is too good to be true. I don't know what to say."

"You don't have to say anything," said Walter beaming with joy.

❖   ❖   ❖

Over the next few years, she gained a certain academic notoriety, which brought her continuous requests to lecture at other universities. She recognized the need for a more challenging role, which also turned out to be financially rewarding for her. Liz took her job seriously, but wanted to have fun also. She ultimately moved onto her yacht full time and enjoyed the different countries she would sail to and give lectures.

It was while Liz was in Europe, lecturing, that she took up painting. She started creating postcard size oils on canvases and sent some of these to her Uncle Walter. When he received them, he was so elated he had them framed and hung them proudly in his study. All of her paintings were just signed "Liz" and a year date.

❖   ❖   ❖

Liz also wanted to do something different so she talked Rick and Walter into letting her take on the Three Forks Restaurant and Lodge project. With the help of Jacques Béarnaise – Walter's General Manager of The Alpinhoff Restaurant in Providence, Rhode Island and the Matterhorn in Manhattan, they began to transform the chain of twelve properties into a resort style lodge. Within two months, she reorganized the executive staff, re-worked the menu and created a new marketing plan to entice a more diversified crowd to stay and eat there.

Chapter

6

Hilda Lowenstein was Walter's housekeeper and cook on his estate. Hilda had also been interred at Sachsenhausen Concentration Camp during the war. She worked as a cook and tailor for Colonel Matthias Theisson when he was stationed at the camp while in the Nazi SS.

After they were released, Walter kept in touch with Hilda and promised to help with her child's education when he could. Her daughter was actually – Liz Hildebrand. Hilda wanted to keep it a secret from Liz that she was her actual mother. All the while, Walter told Liz, at the request of her mother that her parents had died in the war. It was a shock to Liz when she realized that Hilda was her mother. Anna Bowens was her real name, and she changed it when they came to the United States.

In return, Walter had a house built for Hilda and Christopher, her husband, toward the back of his estate and they had the freedom to come and go as they pleased. Hilda and Christopher were very lucky they found each other after the Russians liberated the camp. Since they lived in the same town, they both left together.

❖ ❖ ❖

Jacob Teaubel and his wife Geraldine also came over as immigrants. Walter helped them to immigrate to the United States. Jacob knew Walter when they were working in Sachsenhausen concentration camp. His wife had passed away several years later, and Jacob had no desires to socialize because of the love he had for her.

He was the gatekeeper on Walter's estate. He had a little house close by the gates and monitored everyone that came to see Walter for any reason. Finally, after many years, they finally installed electronic gates, so he wouldn't have to perform that task anymore.

His son was actually – Rick Benedict. He along with Hilda, also wanted to keep it a secret from Rick that he was his actual father. All the while, Walter told Rick that his parents had also died in the war. It was even a bigger shock to Rick when he realized that Jacob was his real father.

"All those years when I would visit Walter," Rick said, "It was you letting me in at the gate."

"Yes it was, and I am sorry to have deceived you," Jacob said. "But at the time it seemed like the right thing to do. We wanted to make sure you had no obstructions going to school and succeeding in the world."

❖ ❖ ❖

Liz and Rick stayed at Walter's house for another week, being acquainted with their parents all over again. It was awkward at first, but by the end of the week, things seemed to settle down. Each had a difficult time with grasping the situation. However, after a day, they were telling Rick and Liz all about how they survived the war and how Walter helped them rebuild their lives.

"I need you to tell me more about my mother," Rick asked. "What was she really like? You have to understand that I grew up thinking I had no family. And all this time...you were right here."

The day moved into night, and Rick was amazed at what his father told him about the war, things that were never written in any history books. It was now midnight and everyone was exhausted with everything that Liz and Rick heard that day about their lives.

"Can we get together some time tomorrow?" Rick asked. "I find this fascinating and how lucky we were in so many ways."

"Yes of course, son," said Jacob, and he walked them to the door as they left.

Chapter

7

In 1942, General Jürgen Fieldmeister was assigned to manage a secret oil refinery in Northern Africa. It wasn't a difficult job, but he found it boring. He had fought many successful campaigns in, Finland, Denmark, Poland, and Russia. He knew as soon as he was promoted to the position of Captain of the Luftwaffe in Munich, that someone in the Nazi Army was watching his performance. He had no family to show off his achievements to and spent his money on girls he found at the bars. He rose in rank very quickly. At one time, he was the youngest General to have been promoted. This was why he was such good friends with Hitler, and was invited numerous times to Hitler's home high in the hills of Berchtesgaden, which was also called Eagles Nest.

Hitler took an instantly liking to him and confided in him about certain aspects of the war that he didn't even talk about with some of his other Generals. Most of his comrades resented him, and he was finally transferred to Northern Africa. This is where he met Dr. Benjamin Fazihd.

❖   ❖   ❖

At some point, he decided he'd had enough of war, even though he had a very safe job. He had ten-thousand soldiers guarding the oil refineries to support General Rommel in Northern Africa. Some of the soldiers started deserting because they couldn't take the heat in the summer. His direct subordinates didn't bother to tell him, because some of them had also left their post. The General didn't seem worried because he was having such a great time. He felt he was on a holiday almost every day. He went to his office in the morning, gave instructions to his aides and then left for the day.

❖   ❖   ❖

Jürgen grew up in the wealthy and affluent part of Berlin. His father was the Mayor of Potsdam, a suburb of Berlin. His mother didn't like Jürgen, because he favored his father instead of her. This started at an early age and until he joined the German Army. He wrote in his memoirs when he was in Northern Africa, that he liked ordering and marching people around. He however did *not* like being marched around and having to take orders.

❖   ❖   ❖

Jürgen had one brother named Erick and one sister named Heidi. They did not share his ideologies about Hitler's new *order*. They tried to make their own way in the world and met with no success. They ultimately fled to Australia in the hopes that they could start a new life, like so many others before them. His parents did not leave, and at some point with his various assignments, nobody contacted him of their passing. He didn't know until several years later when he received a letter from his sister.

Chapter

8

The next day Dr. Fazihd flew to London feeling good that he had an ally with rank, who could help him with his quest. As he was looking out of the airplane window, he thought, *I must secure the ancient papyrus scrolls from the General. This treasure will not be shared with the world.*

He departed from the plane and headed for the taxi stand, but he had a feeling he was being followed. He turned around several times but saw nothing out of the ordinary. The taxi took him directly to the Sir William Sheffield Museum. As he got out of the taxi and stood at the bottom of the forty-five steps leading up into the museum, he always marveled at how dramatic the entire building structure looked. He walked up the wide cement steps and through the massive brass and glass doors. As he strolled through the main lobby, on the highly polished dark green marble floor with white veins, he went directly to the elevator that would take him two floors below the main hallway.

When the elevator stopped on the second floor basement and the door opened, he looked out and suddenly froze in his tracks. He was shocked. He saw wooden crates all around, being packed with items from his and other offices on the same floor.

"Hold on! What is happening here?" shrieked Dr. Fazihd.

"We were just told to box everything up," said the inventory clerk sarcastically, "And put it in storage below, in the fourth floor basement."

Dr. Fazihd slowly entered his office, still in shock and saw his office was almost empty. All his furniture and loose items were packed up. Only his small library of books were still there, neatly stacked on the floor against the wall. He suddenly held his chest, and with a contorted look on his face, collapsed onto the floor. He had had a heart attack

When he woke up a day later, he wondered where he was. He then noticed he was hooked up with tubes and electronic monitoring wires.

He shouted aloud, "Where am I?"

Thomas Benjamin had been sitting in the chair dozing with his glasses sitting halfway down on his nose, when he heard the loud shriek.

"Relax…relax. You're in St Mary's Hospital," Thomas said in a calming tone. "You've had a slight heart attack, but you'll be fine according to the doctor," he spoke casually as he continued working or solving his favorite pastime – crossword puzzles.

"What was the meaning of packing up all my personal belongings?" asked Dr. Fazihd loudly, as he tried to sit up, obviously still in pain and still weak.

"Hold on there, just relax," said Thomas. "The head curator, Dr. Livingsworth, said he needed the space for some new things he'd acquired. He told me that he tried to get in touch with you, but you were in Egypt somewhere. But don't worry all of your crates are neatly marked with your name on them."

"You have no idea what you've done!" said an exasperated Dr. Fazihd, who fell back on his pillow.

❖   ❖   ❖

"I need to get out of here and look through my crates that you stored," Dr. Fazihd said. "There are important papers in those crates that I must have to continue my research."

"Now just sit back and rest," said Thomas. "They will still be there when you're well enough to travel. I'll contact Dr. Livingsworth and make sure he keeps them safe."

The General, he thought. *He may not believe my story and have me killed, thinking I'm trying to keep the treasure for myself.*

"All right then," Dr. Fazihd said. "Can you make sure my crates are delivered to The Heliopolis Museum in Cairo?"

"Yes I can take care of that," Thomas said. "I'll be back in a few days to see how you're doing."

"I guess I have to trust you to take care of my things for me," Dr. Fazihd said.

Even though he didn't know Thomas Benjamin very well, he did not trust him.

❖   ❖   ❖

Dr. Fazihd was in the hospital another two weeks before they released him. He didn't know if he should go back to the museum and confront Dr. Livingsworth, or just go back to Egypt. *I'm not sure my heart can take the confrontation,* he thought, *especially since he didn't like me in the first place. All of my research for the last twenty years – was all in vain.* He finally decided to go back to Cairo and stay as the curator at The Heliopolis Museum.

❖   ❖   ❖

Thomas Benjamin went back to the museum that day.

As soon as he walked in, Dr. Livingsworth asked, "Well how is he doing?"

"He's doing fine," said Thomas. "He'll be there for a few more days."

"I want to give you some additional responsibility for a new section of the museum," Dr. Livingsworth said.

In his haste, he forgot all about Dr. Fazihd and his crates that were in storage.

Chapter

9

Walter Donleavy's first love had always been art. Not just creating paintings, but also owning them. It was one of the things he had always said, and believed – *There will always be only one original.* He first purchased his mansion on the hill overlooking the Diamond Hill Reservoir in northern Providence, Rhode Island. He created a unique place to display his treasures. He had the existing cellar expanded so it went almost the whole length and width of the house. He had it resemble some of the underground bars and wine caverns in Germany. He would go down there, and sometimes spend hours viewing them. He also stored his favorite wines and cognacs in a special climate controlled room.

❖ ❖ ❖

On that particular day, he had read some alarming news in the French newspaper *Le Nouvel Observateur*. They wrote about creating a road show with over three hundred masters from major museums from Europe to the United States. The Masters that were hanging in the *Centre Pompidou, Musée d'Orsay*, and *Musée du Louvre* museums were going to be insured by Lloyds of London. However, before they could be packed and transported to the United States, they had to be appraised and authenticated by a recognized old master art expert, in the event there was an accident that might damage or even destroy them. The museums decided on three renowned *old* master art experts.

The three art experts were hired and started on their arduous task that would take an estimated six months. After about two months, one of the experts, Maurice Protheau, who was working at the *Musée du Louvre,* discovered that one of the paintings was a forgery. The local police and INTERPOL were immediately called in to investigate. After ten days, all three experts assigned to the project, agreed it was a forgery. However, they were no nearer to finding an answer as to who or when this could have been accomplished. They were now in a quandary as to what to do. They had already announced the project and the event for over a year and then of course – the embarrassment to the museum for having forgeries. Each of the Directors of the three museums were notified of the forgery, and that there may be others.

❖　❖　❖

At first, the Director of the *Centre Pompidou* could not believe it. However, he conferred with the other directors at the *Musée d'Orsay*, and *Musée du Louvre* and agreed to continue the appraisal and authentication effort.

"We must continue to insure that there are no other forgeries," he said.

What began as a mere formality for the Insurance company, now had become a crusade to confirm that the other paintings were either authentic or forgeries. As they continued their arduous task, they found five other paintings that were also forgeries. They were replaced with five other masters and the task was complete. It took over nine months, but was finally signed off by Lloyd's of London.

❖   ❖   ❖

Walter had read the final report, which listed the forged paintings. As he sat in his cellar enjoying his favorite tea, he was elated, because three of the paintings listed – he was currently looking at.

I must admit, I did a terrific job when I created those paintings in the 50's, he thought. He remembered how he came about the paintings. He had just entered the United States through New Orleans, coming from Marseilles, France. He'd met with General Mathew Wielding, who was also a close friend to Federico Mariano who lived in Florence.

"Federico tells me you are a true artiste," said the General. "I have three paintings, and don't ask me where I got them from please. I would like you to be a guest in my house for as long as you like and make three perfect forgeries for me. In return, I'll give you a million dollars for all the other paintings that I requested from Federico. What do you say?"

"I'm honored to do this for you," Walter said timidly taken aback by such a generous offer. "However, I may need certain types of paint, brushes, etc. in order to make these copies for you."

"Make me a list and I'll have them here by tomorrow morning," said the General. "Tonight we shall eat like kings. Please… make yourself comfortable."

He spent two months working long hours, and finally completed the task.

"These three paintings will have to dry for another two months, and then they should be fine," said Walter.

"Thank you so very much," the General said pleased with the results. "Is there anything else I can help you with?"

"No, I think I have everything I need for the moment," Walter said. "However, if you could have your driver take me to the train station, I still have a long way to still go."

"I'll take care of it," the General said.

That was the last time he saw the General. They would occasionally send each other Christmas cards, but after a while that stopped.

❖ ❖ ❖

Walter reminisced when he first met Federico Benito Mariano. He ended up in Florence, Italy, where he spent some time just looking at galleries for the type of paintings he liked and found none. It was getting late, the sun was starting to set, and as he crossed the Ponte Vecchio Bridge on the Arno River, he saw the little shops selling their gold and silver jewelry. A small shop at the end of the bridge caught his eye. He was selling what looked like paintings of the old masters. Being curious, he went in and introduced himself to the artist.

Federico was a large man with a huge unkempt, straggly gray beard. He sported a very large purple fedora hat with a long white plume. He almost looked like a pirate in his outfit. He later told him he liked how elegant some of the Three Musketeers looked with their huge hat and plumes. And so that was his trademark look."

They started talking and he learned that he was an artist, but of a different nature. Since he was just closing his store, he invited him to have a drink with him. It was getting late and Walter hadn't anything special to do, so he said yes. They went into his favorite restaurant called the *L'Enoteca Fuori Porta*, which was just outside of Porta San Niccoló on the road up to San Miniato. As he opened the door and walked in, they all greeted him like a long lost son. They had a bottle of wine with cheese and bread and relaxed."

After a little more wine, Benito described the paintings he had at his home – from Degas, Van Gogh, Rembrandt, Rubens, da Vinci, Raphael, and Michelangelo. Walter was skeptical but curious at the same time and didn't quite know how to react. He didn't know whether he was just talking because of the wine or whether he really had these paintings. After another bottle of Sagrantino di Montefalco, he asked me if wanted to see his collection of paintings. It was getting late and he had no place to sleep for the night and thought ...…why not, it could be interesting.

We left the restaurant and started walking up the narrow cobblestone street toward his home. As they walked through the winding streets, that centuries ago were alive with Roman soldiers, they came upon the town square called *Ave del Norte Plaza*. It had a grand fountain with horses and dolphins that seemed to have an endless supply of water. They passed The Church of St. Mary's, and then finally came to his place."

The outside of Federico's home appeared to be a very plain, nondescript looking building. However, when they got closer he noticed a single colossal oak, very weatherworn door with massive and ornate hinges. There didn't appear to be any lock, but as we got closer, he saw two very small holes on the door, just above the massive handles. He took off his Fedora and pulled out a special wire from the inside of his hat lining. Federico very carefully put the wire into the hole with the bottom lock first and the top one next, then he used that same wire in the bottom lock again and the door seemed to very quietly and magically open. He was surprised that this massive door opened so effortlessly and later learned that it was a cantilevered door and the hinges were only for decoration. The door actually sat on two massive metal pins in the floor and in the ceiling. The walls were four feet thick and as the door closed behind us, it made a very soft click and there were no more sounds from the outside. I anticipated a huge house with guards everywhere, but it was just the opposite. It was beautiful, with a unique mix of furniture styles. In some places, the furniture looked like Louis XV furniture and right next to it were modern and contemporary pieces.

❖   ❖   ❖

Walter never knew how the General was able to get the forged paintings to Paris and to the rightful museum. Fifteen years later, three crates arrived from New Orleans at his doorstep. He had Jacob take them down to his cellar. When he opened the first crate, the painting looked familiar to him. There was a note taped to the inside of the crate that read:

"Walter,

You have given me so much pleasure with these paintings. I'm getting old now and I wouldn't want these paintings to go to anybody but you. Oh, by the way. These are the originals. I sent the forgeries to the museum. I just couldn't part with these special works of art."

Regards,

The General

Chapter

10

One cold and dark night, many years ago Walter jumped off Colonel Baryshnikov's private train that was on its way to St Petersburg. He started running in the opposite direction, hoping no one had seen him. As he stopped running and started walking, breathing heavily, he discovered train tracks that split off into a separate spur line. Thinking they were tracks going south, he decided to follow them. It started to snow and if he hadn't taken the Russian Colonel's heavy overcoat and felt hat, he may have frozen to death.

What's this? He thought, as he was following the train tracks. He stopped walking, staring at two massive wooden doors with a heavy chain and oversized padlock securing it. The train tracks continued under the two massive doors. The doors were hinged and the opening to the cave was carved out of solid granite. *What could be stored inside*, he wondered. *It was obviously something to hide a train of some sorts.* The doors were hastily covered with branches from the trees, but most fell down from the heavy snowdrifts.

Walter approached the wooden doors. Each doors was at least twenty-five feet tall and at least ten feet wide. He stood there wondering if he should try to see what was inside. Suddenly in the distance, he heard truck engines coming in his direction echoing through the forest. He quickly ran back into the heavily treed forest, and hid behind a large granite boulder next to a tall fir tree. The truck engines became louder and he knew they would be here shortly. *I wonder if I should just keep walking deeper into the forest, because if they find me, they might kill me,* he thought. He decided to stay where he was. He peeked over the boulder and saw a caravan of six large trucks and two jeeps.

The Oberstleutnant Nazi officer, who was in the lead jeep shouted out, "Let's get this door unlocked, it looks like it may snow again."

Another officer walked up to the double door and unlocked the padlock.

"Let's get this unloaded quickly!" the Oberstleutnant shouted out. "Be careful not to damage any of those crates."

Four of the soldiers had to help pull open the doors they were so heavy. Twenty-some-odd soldiers started to unload the trucks loaded with large wooden-crated items into the cave-like structure. Walter noticed that the names stenciled on the outside of the crates were in large letters and the names were of the biggest art museums in France, Germany and Italy.

Within a few hours, the soldiers finished offloading their truck, closed and padlocked the heavy doors, and drove off. Suddenly it started to severely snow again. *I have to find shelter,* Walter thought. As he walked back towards the double doors, he noticed a small building to the right of the cave, almost hidden by the trees. It looked like a small guard post building. He cautiously approached the building and hoping that no one was in there. He opened the door, peeked in, and found two small cots in the corner. As he walked in and closed the door, he thought, *at least the snow can't come in.* He quickly curled up on one of the cots and fell fast asleep.

Walter woke with a start, and noticed it was daylight outside. Suddenly he realized he hadn't eaten in almost a day and he was now hungry. Unfortunately, there was nothing to eat inside the little hut. However, he did notice that there were various maps tacked onto the walls. He didn't know what they were for, *but what the heck*, he thought. *I'll take all of them with me*, and he left the little guard shack.

It had stopped snowing for the moment, so Walter took that opportunity to start walking down the road, following the route the trucks took. At some point Walter was concerned that the road might be monitored by soldiers. He got off the road and started walking through the thick and heavily blanketed tree branches. A few miles later, he came upon a farmhouse. A man was calmly standing on his porch, bundled up and smoking his pipe, just observing Walter as he slowly walked up to his place.

"Where are you going in this weather?" he asked with a guarded look.

"I'm not sure yet," Walter said. "But I'm sure I'll know when I get there."

Walter stopped and stood in front of the farmhouse and thought to himself, *I must be a sight with this heavy overcoat and nowhere special to go.* He was now feeling very hungry and took a few steps toward the individual standing on the porch.

"Could you spare a slice or two of bread?" Walter asked.

The farmer stood there for a moment and finally said, "Of course. Please come in."

"Thank you very much," Walter said, feeling that luck was on his side today.

"Here….sit down and I'll get you something," the farmer said.

"Again I want to thank you," Walter said as he took of his coat and sat down.

"Margaret…bring some ham, cheese and that fresh rye bread you baked this morning," the farmer said.

Within minutes the table was prepared with so much food, it was overwhelming.

"Where are you from?" asked the farmer.

Walter wasn't quite sure how to answer him, but felt he could trust him and gave him minimal information.

"I was interned at the Sachsenhausen Concentration Camp, which is just outside of Berlin," Walter said. "The Russians liberated what was left of all the people in the camp. Since I had no family, I wanted to get as far away as possible, so I just started walking."

"We were lucky…being so isolated from other farms and houses," said the farmer. "We prayed every day that they would not find us. Our prayers seemed to have been heard."

Walter looked outside through a foggy window and saw it wasn't snowing now, and said, "I want to thank you for your hospitality, but I feel I must go now."

"You are welcome to stay the night," the farmer said.

"Thank you for the offer, but I still have a long way to go," Walter said.

"Then at least take some bread and sausage, for your trip," said the farmer.

Walter hesitated because he was at a loss for words, but said, "Thank you. I will never forget your kindness. One day I hope to repay you."

❖ ❖ ❖

While Walter was sitting in his special room, he was reminded of the maps he took from the guard station, where the train tracks disappeared under the immense doors attached to a carved out granite hillside. Years later, after Walter was settled, he sent a hand written note anonymously, to INTERPOL, along with the maps, and identified where some of the stolen art was located, assuming it was still there. Part of the treasure the Nazi's took from the various museums was hidden in the Berchtesgaden and the Hallein salt mines to insure that they didn't deteriorate. They originally were going to be shipped to the homes of Hermann Goering, Joseph Goebbels and of course Adolph Hitler. However, the war had ended and the paintings never got to them.

❖ ❖ ❖

Walter was now settled in Rhode Island, but he never forgot the kindness he was shown by the farmer and his wife. One day, he flew over to Germany and was lucky enough to find the farm again after all those years. However, the farmer that had invited him in had passed away a few years earlier. Only his wife and two sons were still living there, trying to get by.

"Do you remember me?" Walter asked of the farmer's wife. "You gave me food a long time ago, just as the war was ending."

"Yes, I remember you now," she said, trying to smile.

"I would like to give you some money to take care of you and your boys," Walter said. "I want to thank you, because I told your husband I would never forget what you both did for me." He handed her the money, and again thanked her and left.

As Walter walked down the front steps, he didn't look back. He would have seen a woman, starting to cry wrapped in almost rags, with her two sons standing next to her.

Chapter

11

"It looks like the street is blocked off," Duncan said. "I see a lot of police. And now I see some military people."

Walter just sat, aghast with the situation. He called the General's phone…..but no answer.

"I fear the worst Duncan," he said somberly. "Get us out of here, quickly!"

"Will do," said Duncan, as he made a U-turn on Washington Ave.

As they turning around to leave, there were three very loud *thuds* on the rear window.

"What was that?" Walter asked.

"I don't Mr. Donleavy!" Duncan said. "Just sit tight! I'll get out and see."

"No! Don't get out of the car!" Walter shouted.

"Why not?" asked Duncan.

"The windows are all bullet proof glass!" Walter said. "We're safer in here, than out there."

"Real bullet proof glass?" asked Duncan.

"Yes. I had it installed in this car and my limousine several years ago," Walter said. "Now get us out of here!"

Surprise....surprise, Duncan thought.

❖ ❖ ❖

"How could you miss at this close range!" she said.

"I didn't miss," her partner said casually. "I just didn't know it was bullet proof glass. However, I won't make that mistake again."

She took her sniper rifle apart and neatly arranged it in her briefcase.

"Let's get back to the hotel, she said. "I want to plan our next move."

❖ ❖ ❖

Walter called another close friend on the phone, "Ernie, this is Walter. I know you knew General Howard Metcaff, from your time in the service."

"Yes I did," said Ernie. "He was a special individual and always treated me right. Why do you ask?"

"I would like you to call some of your friends in the Pentagon," Walter said. "Find out about the General for me."

"Why, is he in trouble?" Ernie asked.

"I'm afraid for his life," Walter said. "I was supposed to meet him for lunch. He was going to ask for my help on something that I'm sure was important to him. I'm afraid he's been killed."

"What! What happened?" Ernie asked, shocked.

"That's something I hope you can find out for me," Walter said.

"I'll get right on it," Ernie said, and hung up the phone.

❖ ❖ ❖

Ernie made several calls to some of his most influential military friends in the Pentagon. He found out that nobody could give, or were not allowed to give him any information. They told him that it was now classified and a national security issue.

"You're telling me that nobody knows anything?" Ernie asked frustrated.

"It appears that the people involved or that have anything to do with General Metcaff, are in some type of quarantine," said his friend. "This General Sean Flannigan, who is in charge, has put an extraordinary high-level seal on anything to do with General Metcalff's death."

"Okay…thanks," Ernie said discouraged and hung up.

Wow, this is bigger than Walter knew, Ernie thought. *There has to be somebody that knows something about the accident.* Ernie made a final call to an individual who lived on the *fringes* and knew everything going on in the government.

"Travis, this is Ernie."

"Hi Ernie. Haven't heard or seen you since that time in Guatemala," Travis said.

"Yeah, it has been a long time," said Ernie. "Has your leg healed up enough yet?"

"It never really healed enough to keep it," Travis said cheerfully. "So they took it. But no worries, the VA helped me with that. But you're calling me out of the blue, and I'm sure it's not to wish me a happy birthday."

"You were always very perceptive Travis," Ernie said grinning to himself. "Are you familiar with a General Metcaff?"

"You mean the one that just got killed, *accidentally*?" asked Travis.

"Yeah, that's the one. I need you to dig deep, because it's very important to me," Ernie said. "Also....I need this like yesterday."

"This sounds exciting," Travis said. "I'll call you as soon as I have something."

"One other thing," Ernie said. "Be very careful. You might set off some alarms."

❖   ❖   ❖

Ernie Slater was an ex-CIA operative. He developed his skill during the Vietnam War era when you needed someone to set up electronic surveillance on an individual. Ernie's specialty was to monitor high profile military individuals. His other specialty was as a sniper and detonation expert. He reported to General Phillip Watson, who was responsible for all Asian Pacific Operations.

Each of his surveillance operations was successful. As a result, when he decided to go into private practice, the U.S. Government still used him occasionally as a contractor. He was even allowed to keep his crypto clearance. Ernie worked for the U.S. Government all over the world. His cover was as a news correspondent for a major newspaper in the United States.

Before Ernie left the service, as one of his last assignments, he taught classes at an Army post in Vilsec, Germany to a select few officers from other NATO countries. That's how he met Rick Benedict. He finally figured out that the constant traveling was taking its toll and he stopped working for the Government. However, he still kept the contacts he'd collected over the past twenty years.

Ernie stood about five foot eleven, with blond hair that never seemed to need combing. He had a boyish face, which gave him an advantage sometimes. He had his own business called Slater and Slater Inc. He really was a one-man show as far as his business was concerned. However, he decided that by having two names, it appeared he had a much larger operation. He could choose which clients to take, and he never had any of them come to his office. He always met them at either their home or some out of the way place. He catered to high-level people in organizations.

Soon word got around of his abilities and he had to get an assistant, named Wilber Watkins. He needed someone to manage his business. He got himself a small office, which was primarily to take messages and pay bills – and keep track of Ernie, since he was always working somewhere in the world. He used to be in Ernie's unit, when he was in Vietnam working as an account clerk at headquarters in Phai Tang.

Ernie's personal life was chaotic, in that he had no long-term personal relationships. He had two joys as part of his life. He loved spending time at one of the local bars called *The Last Squadron*. It was mainly military men from the Vietnam era. His other form of relaxation was that he had two girlfriends in Macau at the Red Dragon Casino. It was run by his close friend, Victor Chen.

❖   ❖   ❖

Duncan drove Walter home and didn't stop for anything until they were inside the walls of his estate. Walter got out of the car and went around to the rear window to see what made the *thud-like* noise.

"I think I know what that was," Duncan said as he examined the rear window. "It was a bullet, from a rifle. I've seen these before. It looks like they tried three times. Somebody wants you dead – badly."

"Yes, it looks that way," Walter, said, dismissing it as just another day at the office.

Now Duncan was curious, and Walter didn't want to talk about it.

Chapter

12

Jimmy Hackensack was pacing in his office, dreading the meeting he was going to have with Rocky Cappellini. There was a knock on the door and Jimmy already tense, went to open it.

"Hi Jimmy," said Rocky smiling, holding his arms outstretched. "What's the matter? You don't call, you don't write. Have I offended you?"

"No Rocky," said Jimmy dryly. "I've just been busy, with the restaurant and scheduling the shows. Come on in."

"Yeah, I caught her act last week," said Rocky. "I also saw that they were, four deep at the bar. You must be doing great," he said as he sat down in the leather barrel chair. "Now....you know why I'm here."

"Yes, unfortunately I do," said Jimmy dryly. "I need a little more time. I'm just starting to turn a profit, with the new singer I have."

"Yeah, that was another interesting thing," said Rocky mockingly. "She's a knock-out. I also found out that your new singer….. is actually your sister. We wouldn't want anything to happen to her, would we?"

"Don't threaten me!" Jimmy said menacingly. "You'll get your money, don't worry about it!"

"Oh, I'm not worried," Rocky said casually, "Because I'm your new partner, effective *now*!"

"I don't need a partner!" Jimmy shot back.

"Oh yes you do!" Rocky said loudly. "I need to keep an eye on you and my investment. I need to make sure you don't try to skim any money." He stood up and said, "I'll be seeing you later tonight…partner. I have to get me a new tuxedo if I'm going to help you manage your place. How about if I manage the bar, and you can manage the restaurant and the shows? See you later." He left without letting Jimmy respond.

❖　❖　❖

Dorothy happened to walk into Jimmy's office just as Rocky was leaving.

"Who is that guy?" Dorothy asked.

He didn't answer right away, but finally said, "He's a new guy I hired to watch the bar business," Jimmy said, as he looked away from her nervously.

"Jimmy! I thought we were going to talk about any new people to hire," Dorothy asked firmly.

"Well I forgot," Jimmy said coldly.

"There's something going on here Jimmy, and I want the truth!" Dorothy exclaimed. "What is it?"

Jimmy turned to look at her and said, "You might as well know it. I was doing well and I got cocky and gambled a little. Then the business took a turn for the worst. I borrowed money from him and I haven't paid all of it back yet."

"How much do you still owe him?" Dorothy asked, walking boldly closer to his desk.

Jimmy was stammering around and finally said, "About fifty thousand. "Look, we're doing well now and I should have enough to pay him back soon."

"Jimmy…..how could you!" Dorothy said. "After all we've been through to get this place started! Why wouldn't you tell me?"

"I was too embarrassed, and I thought I could take care of it myself," Jimmy said, turning away from her.

Dorothy stormed out of his office, flushed with anger as she slammed the door behind her.

Jimmy sat in his overstuffed executive chair, trying to figure out how he could get rid of Rocky. *I have to kill him somehow*, he thought.

❖ ❖ ❖

When Jimmy came back home from Viet Nam, he was in terrible mental and physical shape. Dorothy knew that her brother Jimmy was not doing well at the VA Hospital, but didn't know he had left. She spent months tracking him down. When she finally found him, she took him home to live with her. After a lot of private therapy, she was able to help him get his life turned around. A year later, Jimmy and Dorothy were able to open a small seafood restaurant called it *The Seafood Peddler*. She'd been singing there ever since. Her singing was a draw and twice they'd had to expand the place because people were waiting outside in long lines, not just to eat – but also to hear her sing.

Chapter

13

Walter was a very distinguished looking individual, with his full coiffed silver gray hair. His beard and mustache were always perfectly groomed. He stood five-foot-eleven, with steel blue eyes that melted the hearts of many women, and were intimidating to others. He had a smile that would light up a room, which he used sparingly and only when it was advantageous. He always dressed impeccably and often wore Brooks Brothers three-piece suits, with a royal blue silk handkerchief in his breast pocket – his signature look. He primarily worked out of his home and converted his magnificent library into his office.

He was a long-term planner, and always felt that information was the key to being successful. He was meticulous in everything he did. Over a short period of time, he had purchased outright newspapers, magazines, radio stations, and several television stations, including a communication network in Europe called *Balgonai Lek'tronics*. He also owned one of the most exclusive

Persian-style rug companies called the *Balducci Couture* in Tel Aviv, Israel. Each of his enterprises was doing well because he provided very lucrative incentives to his executives.

People knew very little about Walter, and that was how he liked it. In the financial world, he was almost invisible and he went to great lengths to keep it that way. He typically paid a little more for the companies he wanted to purchase, and this eliminated the bickering and negotiating of the sale, where deeper research and investigation might expose Walter to revealing more about himself.

❖ ❖ ❖

He had a keen eye for buying a business he wanted. He would have Fred perform very in-depth analysis not just about the company, but also the principals of the company. This had paid off handsomely on several occasions for Walter.

Chapter

14

Liz received a phone call from Francisco Romano, who was the manager of the Coeur D' Alene and Clearwater, Idaho, Three Forks Restaurant & Lodge chain.

"Do you remember those two guys you fired from the two restaurants in Cody and Cheyenne, Wyoming?" Francisco asked.

"Yes. What about them?" Liz asked curiously. "Are they giving us any trouble?"

"I heard through some of my friends at the other restaurants," Francisco said, "that they're hanging around and bothering the patrons."

"Well, we can't have that," Liz said. "I'll make preparations to fly up to Cody in the morning and see what's going on. Thanks Francisco," she said and she hung up.

I guess I should have seen this coming, she thought. *However, I won't let that happen again.*

❖   ❖   ❖

Francisco Romano was originally a short-order cook on a battle ship stationed primarily in Hawaii. He finally got into communications and ended up spending the rest of his tour of duty at the Kaneohe Marine Base on Oahu, Hawaii. He had received numerous commendations for making communication improvements that went all the way to the Pentagon level. For his latest improvement, he received a commendation and a promotion out of it. However, since he was drafted, and felt he had no real future, he didn't re-enlist and left the Marines. He stood five-foot-ten, was muscular from when he worked in the landscaping industry at home. When he left the service, he restarted his own landscaping business and was quite success-ful. But that wasn't enough for him, so he went back to being a cook, which later turned into a chef's position in a larger diner in Seattle. He ultimately started his own restaurant called the *Brass Teapot*. He sold it, made a handsome profit and bought into the Three Forks Restaurant and Lodge as a managing part-ner in Coeur d' Alene.

After the chain of restaurants was sold to Monarch Enterprise Corporation, Liz decided to make Francisco the managing Director of both of the Three Forks Restaurant and Lodge in Idaho.

❖   ❖   ❖

Liz flew up to Cody, Wyoming to find out exactly what these two people were doing to her place to cause Francisco some concern. There was another individual several seats behind observing her. When she got off the airplane, she went to the car rental agency as she had done numerous times before, and drove over to the Three Forks Restaurant and Lodge. She parked in front of the restaurant, sat there and looked around. Suddenly Francisco walked out to greet her.

"Hello, Mrs. Benedict," smiled Francisco. "I thought I should fly over and meet with you. They left about an hour ago, but here are some of the flyers they're distributing inside and at the lodge doors."

"Let me find out where they live and I'll go and pay them a visit," Liz said. "I told them that I meant business when I fired them. I guess they thought I was kidding. I don't want you involved in this – I'll take care of it."

"But you may need some help with these guys," Francisco said.

"Do you see that guy in the blue car across the parking lot?" Liz said, pointing. "He'll help me, if I need any help. Don't worry I'm not going to kill them. However, I will put the fear of God into them and this time make sure they don't bother us again."

"Okay, if you say so," said Francisco, wondering how she was going to handle this.

"In the meantime, let's get something to eat," Liz said happily. "Anything good to eat around here? And don't worry....I play nice...most of the time." She grinned.

❖ ❖ ❖

As Liz and Francisco ate dinner, he told her about what had been going on in Coeur de' Alene.

"I mentioned there was an opportunity for sponsoring events," said Francisco. "Laura has been working feverishly to land some big talents."

"That sounds promising," Liz said. "I guess the next thing you're going to bring up is the building to house all of those events."

"Well....yes I am," he said.

"Have we found out what it's going to cost us yet?" Liz asked.

"I contacted an architect who gave me some preliminary plans," he said.

"Let me see those plans, along with this is going to cost us," Liz asked. "Then give me a list of the events that we may potentially attract. I'll take these plans home and let you know in about a week."

Chapter

15

Liz went to sleep that night a little pumped up for the next day. She was up very early and waited outside in her car for morning to come. Finally, after sitting in the car for over two hours, she saw a dirty, rusty-looking pick-up truck drive up to the restaurant. Her two *friends* parked sloppily in front, using two spaces, she noticed. They got out and walked into the restaurant. She got out and walked inside about ten minutes later, and went directly to their booth and slid in alongside one of them.

"Hello boys," Liz said smiling. "Surprised to see me? I understand you're bothering my customers."

They were caught off guard, and said, "What are *you* doing here? We're just going to have a little breakfast," looking at the menu intently.

"I was in the area and thought I would stop by and see how things are working," Liz said. "I need to warn you two boys about something. Do you see that person at the counter over there, with the sleeveless shirt? He's a friend of mine. I'm getting ready to sell him a small stake in my restaurant business. He was just released from prison in Florida. He almost killed a man with his bare hands, but got off early with good behavior because he's not right in the head. You see, he used to live on a *gator* farm. One day one of the *gators* made a mistake and got too close to him. The gator got within three feet of him and was about to grab his leg. He turned around, grabbed the jaws and forced it open until its jaw was broken. Then the Game warden tried to arrest him.... well you can guess the rest. He can bench press four hundred pounds."

"You're just trying to scare us," he said sarcastically.

"No, I'm actually trying to save your lives," Liz said. "I told him he could come in here every day, seven days a week, and whenever he wants. In return, he promised to call me every time he sees either of you around here. I've given you fair warning. Now, I would like to introduce him to you in case you're not sure I'm serious."

Liz hailed him to come over from the bar and stand next their booth.

"Hi Kadar," Liz said smiling. "I want you to meet my two *friends* I want you to keep an eye on for me."

"Hello boys," Kadar said, smiling with all yellow teeth, with three of his teeth missing. "Anybody want to arm wrestle me?"

They took one look up at him and slowly started inching their way out of the booth.

"You didn't finish your breakfast," Liz said as they slowly stood up.

Kadar said, "Here, let me walk you outside."

They looked at Kadar, who was six feet-four and had a sleeveless shirt on, that showed his enormous arms. Each arm had a massive tattoo with a girl's name on each bicep.

After they left, Francisco walked over to Liz and said, "Where did you find that guy? He's as big as a house and just plain butt-ugly."

"When I was at the airport," Liz said. "I asked if he'd like to make a hundred bucks and have a fantastic steak dinner on me. He agreed, so I gave him directions and told him to meet me here at seven, o'clock. This is a one-time deal, but I gave him your name and you can make him the same offer, if you ever need him."

"That's fantastic!" he exclaimed, "and we didn't even have to break any furniture or hit anybody. Thanks again."

"Give me a call anytime Francisco," Liz said, "We *really* want to make this and the other restaurants and lodges great places for people to want to come."

❖ ❖ ❖

Liz left the next morning and was on her way back to Monarch Ranch. She felt good, and didn't even have to shoot anybody. *This is more fun than I could ever imagine,* she thought to herself. *We're going to have to set up something more permanent, so I don't have to fly up here every time,* she thought. *With the two Indian Casinos finished, and almost open for business, we might need some special security.*

"Hi Steve. This is Liz. How are you these days?"

"Well hello there Liz," Steve said. "Happy to hear from you. Haven't talked to you in a while. How are things going for you and your new restaurant business?"

"That's what I want to talk to you about," she said. "With the twelve new restaurants I manage, we may need someone available who can cover the four states they're located in. I know you're considering moving your main office to Sausalito. What about setting up an office in the Billings, Montana area?"

"I'm sure I can arrange that," Steve said. "Are you having any troubles at the moment?"

"Nothing I can't handle for the time being," she smiled. "But you never know. Then of course, we have the two casinos opened for business. And don't forget, we now have a meat processing plant at the Billings restaurant site."

"Wow, you guys have been busy," said Steve amazed. "I think we can do something pretty quick. I'll let you know when I'm ready."

"Thanks Steve," Liz said, and hung up.

Chapter

16

It was late at night when Janus Parn left his office in Tallin, Estonia and was on his way home. He was still terrified that he'd been found out. He had a car, but was nervous about what had happened recently. He decided to take the street trolley instead, which was only two blocks away.

I wish it were closer, he thought. As he got on the trolley late that night, it was raining lightly. The streets were glistening with the few streetlights still working. There was no moon out that night, just the occasional streetlight. Some of the street-lights still had not been fixed since the war. It was also the last ride he could take before they shut down the trolley for the night. He sat there, kept his head down and coat collar turned up. He felt that the three people sitting across from him were all staring at him. The reason they were looking at him, was that he was wearing a fine wool coat, with a large fur-like hat and leather gloves. The clothes they wore were ordinary and tattered.

I have to contact Bernhard, he thought as he sat there. *He would know what to do. It still seems so strange that Alfred would call me after so many years, unless he knows something.*

The trolley had stopped moving and the conductor yelled out, "This is the end of the line." Suddenly, he came out of his trance, and realized that he had gone way beyond where he should have gotten off. It was now almost nine o'clock and he hurriedly got off the trolley and walked back the five blocks toward his house. All the while looking around, in case someone was following him.

❖   ❖   ❖

Bernhard Krueger was the name he used when he was a high-level banker at Reichsdeutche Bank located in Bayern, Germany. He changed his name during the war to Matthias Theisson when he was in the Nazi Army and working at Sachsenhausen Concentration Camp. He managed the special section at the camp that was responsible for creating counterfeit English bank notes, passports, birth certificates and a host of other items. He was the second person Hitler had put in charge of this project. The other senior officers in Hitler's inner circle didn't like Bernhard, because he was automatically promoted to the position of Colonel for this venture.

He knew he could not fail, or he would go the way that his predecessor did – with a bullet to the head. Bernhard wasn't going to fail. He also found an opportunity for himself as well. That was where he met Alfred Berger, who later changed his name to Walter Donleavy.

❖   ❖   ❖

Walter knew Janus lived in Tallin, Estonia. Janus was one of the people he'd bonded with while he was at the concentration camp. He was one of two photoengravers Walter was using to produce the English banknotes. Janus always felt paranoid and that made him vulnerable, because the guards always picked on the group and pushed them around. The guards were jealous because these prisoners were treated better than they were. Only when the Colonel was in the camp, did the abuse stop. As a result, Janus had a difficult time trusting anybody. He started becoming more suspicious as time went on.

He told one of the guards something about the other photoengraver. When the Colonel left for the day, the guards took the individual from the barracks late at night, and beat him to death. After that, the guards didn't bother him anymore – because he was now considered an informant. The other inmates knew about the killing, but didn't say anything to the Colonel, for fear of reprisals.

Colonel Theisson approached Janus one day, because he knew of his paranoia, and made a deal with him.

"I don't trust Alfred to make the additional money and keep quiet about it," The Colonel said, even though Alfred had already agreed to print the extra money.

However, the Colonel was greedy, so he'd made a second deal with Alfred at the same time.

❖   ❖   ❖

"Why are you calling me, Janus?" asked Bernhard. "You got your share of the money and I gave you a passport to get you back to Estonia. What else do you want?"

"Out of the blue, I received a phone call from Alfred Berger," said Janus.

"What?" Bernhard said stunned. "How did he get your phone number?"

"He said he ran across my name in some type of ledger he found," Janus said.

"That's impossible!" Bernhard said. "He couldn't have called you. I made a deal with Colonel Baryshnikov of the Russian Army to take Alfred with him. I even created this plausible story for him that Alfred knew where there were millions of the English banknotes hidden."

"I just don't know what he wants," Janus said quietly. "It may have been just an innocent call and I may just be overly worried."

"Let's not do anything hasty for the time being," Bernard said. "If he calls you again, let me know," and he hung up the phone.

❖   ❖   ❖

Janus hung on the phone and just stared at his desk at home, still trying to figure out why Alfred had called him.

"Helena," said a terrified Janus as he put down the phone. "We may have to move again!"

"But why?" she asked with a perplexed look on her face. "What has happened that we have to move again?"

"It's something that happened during the war when I was in the concentration camp," Janus said. "I don't want to talk about it any further than that."

"But all our friends and family are living here," she said bewildered by his sudden strange request. "What will we tell them?"

"I don't know," Janus said. "Maybe this will all blow over, but I just want us to be prepared."

"Can you at least tell me what it is you are afraid of?" she asked.

"No, I cannot!" said Janus defiantly.

Chapter

17

I wonder what this could be all about, Bernhard thought trying to think back to his time at Sachsenhausen. *I can't believe Alfred is still alive. How could Alfred have found out about the deal I made with Colonel Baryshnikov?* Bernhart now had to consider that he'd possibly been found out. The scandal at the bank would ruin him and even worse, they could still put him on trial as an officer in the Nazi Army. All he could see in his mind was the Nuremburg Nazi Tribunal war crimes that he narrowly escaped…….all over again. *The only thing I can do is to find Alfred,* he thought, *and kill him…and quickly.* He contacted an old friend, Ulrich Pasternoff, who was in charge of one of another concentration camp. He had also done well with the counterfeit English Banknotes. *He may have a contact I could use,* he thought.

❖   ❖   ❖

"Ulrich. This is Bernhard Krueger."

"Hello Bernhard," said Ulrich. "How have you been? It has been a long time since we had a drink and talked about the old days. You must come around to my home in Baden-Württemberg."

"I'd like that very much," said Bernhard. "However, I have something more pressing. I have a potential problem that I hope you can help me with."

"Of course. What is it?" Ulrich said.

"I would rather discuss this in person if you wouldn't mind," said Bernhard. "I will take the next available train."

"That's fine. Let me know your schedule and I will have you picked up at the station," Ulrich said, and hung up.

❖   ❖   ❖

This is terrific, Bernhard thought. *I hope he can help me with this problem.*

"Monica, I will be gone for a day," he said, taking only his briefcase. As he walked to his car, he felt a sense of relief that he has someone who may be able help him. *I hope Janus is not going to create any more problems for me,* he thought.

❖   ❖   ❖

Ulrich put the phone down and sat wondering. *Why all of a sudden does he want to see me?* He opened his humidor and he took out one of his cigars. He always felt he could think better while smoking one. He held it his hands, feeling and then smelling it. He finally clipped the end, and with one of his long matches, lit his cigar. He puffed on it until he could see the glow of the ember at the end.

"Hellena. Please come in here," he said nonchalantly.

Almost on cue, Hellena opened his office door and walked in.

Hellena was his personal aide. She was young and statuesque and always wore dresses that were very body hugging, bright multi-colored, and in good taste.

"Yes Mr. Pasternoff," she answered politely.

"Be ready to pick up someone at the Baden Hauptbahnhof as soon as I find out what time he's arriving," Ulrich said.

"I'll be ready, just let me know,' she said as she walked back to her office.

Ulrich always loved to watch Hellena walkaway towards her office. *She has that interesting sway with her hips,* he thought smiling. *Apollo had taught you well.*

❖   ❖   ❖

Bernhard had to be careful how he talked to Ulrich. He had heard about his possible connections with a group that would kill anyone….if the price was right. He often wondered how he was able to buy into a major electronics firm, even though it took years. Suddenly the previous owner mysteriously died in his sleep.

❖   ❖   ❖

Ulrich Pasternoff was a Major in the Nazi Army in charge of one of the concentration camps in Poland. Perceptive enough to see that the war was not going well, he had already concluded that when the war ended, he could be caught and go to prison or even hanged. One day, he decided to visit another camp on the premise of some type of meeting. He was about twenty miles out of the camp on a deserted road, when he pulled out his German Luger pistol and shot his driver in the head. He dumped the body deep in the forest. He then drove to where his wife and three children were staying, picked them up and traveled to a safe house off the beaten path in Baden- Württemberg.

He had known Bernhard Krueger when they were in school and knew he was in charge of the English Banknote counterfeiting program, known as Operation Bernhardt. They had already planned to have them print an additional two hundred thousand, fifty-pound banknotes, to be used to start their new life.

He changed his name and looks, stayed quiet for ten years, and then bought into a major electronics company in Germany, called Brandenburg Electronic. He ultimately rose to prominence and became the president of the company. Once there, he vowed that nothing was going to get in his way to change that.

Chapter

18

Two days later Bernhard arrived at the Baden-Wurttemberg train station. It was noon with clear skies as he walked down the concrete steps to the curb. He noticed a blonde female smartly dressed in a chauffeur's uniform, holding up a sign with his last name on it.

"Thank you for picking me up," said Bernhard pleased, as he got into a new Mercedes. He noticed it had tinted glass on both sides of the back seat and the rear window.

"It is my pleasure," said the driver and tipped her hat. "Sit back and relax, we have about an hour before we get there."

They drove off onto the E45 highway. She drove for about thirty minutes, and then got off the highway to a smaller more secluded road. The chauffeur stopped the car, turned around and without any hesitation, shot Bernhard twice in the forehead. She got out of the car, took the body, dumped it into a previously dug hole, and covered it up.

"It's done," the driver said into her cell phone, as she walked back to her car.

"Thank you Hellena," said Ulrich. "You can come back home now, and we can have dinner at the *Ratskeller*, if you like."

❖ ❖ ❖

Nobody came looking for Bernhard because he hadn't notified anyone where he was going. His wife knew he often went on unscheduled business trips for long periods of time. Two days later Hellena went to Bernhard's home.

"Mr. Krueger has been in a bad accident," Hellena said. "He has regained consciousness and has asked for you and your two sons to come to the hospital."

"Of course, we will come," said Mrs. Krueger, frantic that he may be badly hurt.

Hellena helped them into her car, drove out of town and killed all three – execution style. She dumped the bodies over a cliff that was inaccessible.

"Part two of your plan is done," Hellena said into the cell phone.

"Good," said Ulrich. "Now there is nothing to connect him to my organization. Apollo has taught you well my dear. Thank you." And he hung up.

❖ ❖ ❖

A few days later Janus tried to call Bernhard, but got no answer. He tried several more times, also without success. *I wonder if I started something by calling Bernhard,* he thought. *Maybe it's best if I go visit him in person.*

"Mariana," Janus called out.

"Yes Janus," she answered.

"I'm going to visit a client in Baden-Baden," Janus said. "I'll be back in two days. Please pack my small suitcase."

Mariana was worried, because Janus did not normally visit clients anymore. Nevertheless, she packed him a small bag as he requested, and a sandwich for the road she put in his valise. Janus picked up his bag and left. His wife was staring out of the front window, through the lace curtain, watching him walk down to the bench where the trolley would pick him up and take him to the Baltic Jam train station.

❖　❖　❖

Janus got on the trolley, still concerned that he was being followed. The trolley stopped close to the train station. He got off, went to the ticket counter and purchased a ticket. He went directly to the train platform and got on the train. *I won't be settled down until I see Bernhard,* he thought as he handed his ticket to the conductor. However, the conductor took a parting glance at him as he left to go to the next row of passengers.

Janus caught that glance and began to worry. He moved to an aisle seat, in case he had to leave in a hurry. Nothing happened for the next forty-five minutes. He got off the train and almost ran to the next ticket counter to buy a ticket to continue his travel to Baden-Baden. The rest of his trip was uneventful.

Chapter

19

Ernie received a phone call from Travis.

"Ernie, what I'm about to tell you will blow your socks off?" Travis said eagerly, trying to contain himself. "I almost didn't believe it myself. But you can't just make this stuff up."

Over the course of an hour, Travis told Ernie how General Metcaff and General Flannigan were supposed to be on some type of special assignment, when they were in North Africa thirty years ago.

"I doubt if that was a real military operation, though," Ernie said.

"That's still a question that I couldn't get answered," Travis said. "But I can tell you this. It has more than just those two Generals now involved. The Egyptian Government is involved also, but I don't know how, and to what level. The security is so tight on this that even *I'm* having trouble getting information."

"Now that part lends some credibility to the story," Ernie said.

"One part is that there is some type of papyrus document showing where they think a small pyramid was buried by the sands, somewhere in Egypt," Travis said. "At one time Hitler was supposed to have acquired an old papyrus scroll from somebody. Then this German General Fieldmeister, who was supposed to be a good and close friend of Hitler, somehow got it from him, but how, is also not quite clear yet either."

"So where is this papyrus document today?" asked Ernie.

"That part is *also* still not known," Travis said. "It may have been sold by General Fieldmeister to the Egyptian Government, since he appears not to have the document. Don't forget… this is only to locate the pyramid, which is supposed to be the tomb of this supposed, Princess. That's all I know about it."

"Thanks Travis. I owe you one," Ernie said, and hung up.

That's such a fantastic story that I just heard, Ernie thought. *However, it may just be true.*

❖   ❖   ❖

"Hi sweetheart," Steve said as he walked towards Dorothy.

"Hi Steve," Dorothy said, looking away from Steve so he wouldn't see her tears.

"What's the matter?" he asked sounding worried. "You look upset about something."

Dorothy looked at Steve, tears forming in the corner of her eyes. No matter how many times she tried to dry her eyes, they just came back.

"It's Jimmy," Dorothy said unhappily. "He's got himself into some trouble with a bookie, and gambling. Now, because he hasn't paid it all back, the guy made himself a *partner* in the bar business."

Steve tried to calm her down and was trying to figure out how to help them. He knew Dorothy wouldn't want him to get involved.

"Maybe it'll work itself out," Steve said trying to sound positive. "How much is he into him for?"

"I don't want to get you involved," Dorothy said. "This is Jimmy and my problem, and we'll deal with it," and rushed off to get ready for her show that night.

I have to see what this is all about, Steve thought.

❖   ❖   ❖

That night Steve came back to the *Seafood Peddler* and sat at the bar observing. He knew all the bartenders and they all knew him – but not what he was capable of doing. He spotted the new guy right away, because he was the only person wearing a tuxedo behind the bar. What actually made him stand out even more was that he had several gold rings with diamonds on each hand. And, he was wearing an expensive Rolex watch.

Steve overheard him say to the other bartenders, "From now on beer is eight bucks, wine is ten bucks, and hard liquor is twelve bucks."

"But I didn't get an approval from Mr. Hackensack," said the bartender.

"Since I'm the new bar manager," Rocky said. "You now work for me, and I said these are the new rates!"

"Well okay. But our customers aren't going to like it," said the bartender, wondering why Jimmy hadn't told him himself.

"You let me worry about that!" Rocky said defiantly.

Steve was in earshot and heard everything.

He called the bartender over and said, "Give me a beer please."

The bartender looked up, saw it was Steve, and said, "Sorry Steve…but we now have new rates as of five minutes ago," looking back towards Rocky.

"That's okay. I don't want you to get in trouble," Steve said.

❖　❖　❖

Steve nursed that beer for the next several hours, while watching Dorothy perform her first set of songs. When she wasn't performing, he watched Rocky as he paraded around as if he was the ringmaster at a circus.

Rocky walked behind the bar and went to both cash registers. He took money out, and started to leave.

The other bartender saw him and asked, "Hey…what are you doing?"

"You have too much cash here," Rocky said. "I'm taking this and putting it in the safe," he said. However, he didn't go to Jimmy's office – he went outside.

After he did this a second time, Steve followed him outside to see what he was doing. He saw him leaning against one of the cars smoking a cigar.

Steve walked up to him, "Nice little racket you've got going on here," he said.

"Who the hell are you?" Rocky yelled out. "I'm Jimmy's partner..."

"No you're not," Steve said, not letting him finish his sentence. "Why don't you consider this you're severance pay and never come back? Don't call him, or write him or contact him in any other way."

"Oh I see," Rocky said in a snarly voice. "He's got himself some muscle," and waved to a car parked in the lot. Two rather large men stepped out and walked towards them like linebackers in a football game. "I've got more muscle. So beat it, before my friends take you apart and you become a boat anchor in the bay!"

"I don't think so," Steve said, and kept talking until Rocky's two friends were in reaching distance. Suddenly Steve turned and kicked one of them in the groin hard, and he went down, groaning rather loudly, as he was rolling around the ground. He hit the other person in the face, and you could hear cartilage crunch in his nose. He also went down with blood all over his face and clothes. All of this was over in less than thirty seconds.

"Now....you were saying?" as Steve turned back to Rocky.

"I'm not going away that easily!" said Rocky, as he was about to reach into his inside coat.

"I wouldn't do that," Steve said, as he grabbed his wrist, "Unless you want to find a new place to wear your hat."

Rocky, was now furious, because nobody ever talked to him that way, continued to reach into his coat and started to pull out a gun. Steve punched him so hard, and with such force, that it lifted him up and he landed spread-eagled on the hood of the car.

Steve picked up the guy, still holding his crotch and said, "Take your friend and your boss home and never… I mean never…. ever, come back here."

He watched him pick up his friend with the broken nose and, limping, put him in the back seat. Meanwhile Steve went through Rocky's pockets, took out the cash he'd taken and his wallet. His friend came back, picked up Rocky, who was still out cold with blood all over his face and tuxedo and put him in the back seat. Steve watched them drive off. He picked up the gun Rocky dropped, took out the clip, emptied the chamber and threw them into the dumpster.

Steve walked back into the *Seafood Peddler,* and took up his same seat close to the bar. He ordered another beer and gave the bartender a rather large tip. The bartender thought he knew what happened, but didn't say anything. He changed the price of drinks back to what they were before. Steve never mentioned this to Dorothy or Jimmy.

Chapter

20

Upon her graduation, Liz's Uncle Walter, drove her down to the harbor in Providence. He presented her with a *Ferretti 74* yacht, complete with a full-time captain, Stephen Weisen.

"Well, what do you think?" asked Walter. "She has twin diesel engines, travels at twenty-six knots full speed, and includes a complete kitchen and cooking system. It also has a washer and dryer and could easily sleep six."

Liz was in disbelief and was getting ready to ask, *what am I going to do with a boat*, but caught herself and didn't say anything.

They went on board and looked at the living room, bedroom, and galley area. She was so happy that tears ran down her cheeks.

She finally said, "Uncle Walter, this is just absolutely beautiful, but I can't afford this."

"This is a present for doing so well in school," Walter said, "except you have to buy your own clothes and food. Stephen

Weisen is your full-time ship's captain and will take care of everything, including all maintenance requirements."

"Come Elizabeth," said Walter, "I'd like you to meet Stephen Weisen, your captain for your ship."

As they boarded her yacht, Stephen came out of the galley area to meet them.

"Hello Elizabeth," said Stephen. "It is a pleasure to finally meet you. Welcome aboard."

Liz looked up and saw a tall man, with blond hair sticking out of a sailors cap, wearing a white T-shirt and white pants wearing deck shoes.

"Hi Stephen," Liz said, feeling euphoric at not only the boat, but also a handsome man.

"I know what you were thinking," said Stephen. "You were expecting some old grizzled, scraggly beard man, with a parrot on my shoulder."

"To be honest, I didn't know what to expect," said a smiling Liz. "This has been such an incredible day, that I'm just overwhelmed by all of this."

Liz was so overjoyed, that she ran up to her uncle, wrapped her arms around him, and said, "Oh thank you so much Uncle Walter."

"You're very welcome," said Walter.

❖ ❖ ❖

Steve Weisen graduated from Annapolis in 1973, served several tours of duty in Vietnam, Korea, and finished out his service in Germany. When he finished his tour, Walter was waiting for him with a special job. He'd excelled in all the techniques of managing a ship. He was also an expert in hand-to-hand combat, knew how to use almost any weapon, and became proficient in counter-terrorism. He owed Walter since he also helped his parents come over from Austria.

At first, Steve didn't think he could live and work in such a mundane environment as a ship's captain, especially after doing tours in Vietnam and in Korea, plus many *black-ops* missions. He felt this might be too tame for him.

"Give it a try for a couple of months," Walter said to him, "and if you're still having trouble adjusting, I'll understand and will get someone else."

However, after being at sea for a short while, Steve decided he liked it a lot more than he'd expected. He liked sailing, especially in the Mediterranean. He felt he was on a permanent long-term vacation and after three months told Walter, "I've got to be crazy not to do this. Thanks, Walter, for the opportunity."

"One of your other responsibilities," said Walter looking more serious. "Your other job is looking out for Liz, like being a bodyguard. I consider all of you as my children and as such, you must take care and look out for each other."

❖   ❖   ❖

Rocky Cappellini was a small-time hood who always had an angle going. He got started by organizing a group of people to his poker game. If he liked you, he would take some of your money one week, and the next week, he would give some of it back. His games were all rigged. He was a charming individual on the surface, but as vicious as they came. He was a flashy dresser, always wearing lots of jewelry. Nobody knew it, but most of it was fake, except his Rolex watch, which he won from one of his previous players. He was about six feet tall, with a full head of black hair, which always shined like a just-waxed car.

He dropped out of school early, and did a short stint in the Army, but was kicked out on a *section 8. He* went into the loan shark business, which was very lucrative. From there, he moved into being a bookie, which gave him that notoriety he'd been searching for while climbing the ladder of crime. He still ran card games in the back room of a garage his brother owned.

Chapter

21

Walter's cell phone rang. "Hello?"

"It's me, Ernie. I'm sorry to tell you this, Walter, but General Metcaff *is* dead."

"It is as I suspected," Walter said somberly. "How did he die?"

"It appears it was a traffic accident of some type," Ernie said. "However, there is a lot more to this."

"Why do you say that?" asked Walter.

"Within literally just a few minutes the military converged on the scene, declared it a national security issue, and took over the investigation," Ernie said.

"That is peculiar," Walter said. "Do you know who took over the investigation?"

"Yes I do," Ernie said. "His name is Brigadier General Sean Flannigan."

"I have a feeling that since the military was so quick to respond," Walter said, "He must have been under surveillance for some time. I suspect it must be something from his past."

"I also got a call from another friend of mine," Ernie said. "And this is where the story takes a unique twist."

"What did he tell you?" Walter asked, tiring of having to pull the information from Ernie.

"You are not going to believe this," Ernie said excitedly. "Metcaff and Flannigan go way back to their West Point days. They were both commissioned as Lieutenants at the same time. In 1952, they were assigned to Northern Africa, specifically to Egypt, to perform some type of clean-up duty after the Nazi Army surrendered. They happened to stumble upon a high-ranking Nazi general still alive and living there in the hospital. His name was General Jürgen Fieldmeister. He was dying from a variety of illnesses and even tried to commit suicide, but failed twice. However, when he was in the hospital, he was delirious and rambling. He kept talking about a crown of solid gold with jewels that was given to a Princess. He supposedly had a papyrus scroll he somehow stole from Hitler that showed where the pyramid was located. However, what's interesting is that later they found out she was actually King Sekhemkhet's blood sister."

"Now, that, I find very interesting," Walter said. "But what does this have to do with the two generals?"

"Evidently they believed his story and started to look into it," Ernie said. "They were still in the Army and used this as a smoke-screen to continue their search. There was another individual named Dr. Benjamin Fazihd, the head curator of a small museum in Egypt named The Heliopolis Museum. He was also at one time the assistant curator of the Sir William Sheffield Museum in London, England. He was supposed to have the actual papyrus scrolls, which would lead them to where the secret door to the pyramid is located, which is supposed to be the tomb of this so-called Princess and the crown. Then there is another story circulating that in 1934, the pyramid and burial chamber was actually found intact, but the crown was already gone."

"I find that interesting and am curious, that Howard would get himself involved with something like this," Walter said.

"Well that may be so," Ernie said. "However, when Dr. Fazihd flew back to the London Museum he had a heart attack. At the same time, they told him his services were no longer needed. They crated up all of his things, assuming he would come back to claim them – but he never did. He, in the meantime, decided to go back to Cairo and tell General Fieldmeister that the documents were lost."

"I'm very familiar with the Sir William Sheffield Museum in London," said Walter. "What happened after that?"

"When Dr. Fazihd flew back to Cairo, he told General Fieldmeister that they packed up all his belongings and fired him," Ernie said. "The General, while delirious with rage, went on a rampage and killed him. From then on, the General was hiding somewhere in the city, until your two friends accidentally found him in the hospital."

"That's very interesting," Walter said in a flat tone. "Anything else Ernie?"

"No. That's it for now," Ernie said. "But I'll let you know if I find out anything else."

"Thanks Ernie," Walter said, and hung up his phone.

❖ ❖ ❖

Walter's next call was to Fred Tremaine.

"Hello Fred. This is Walter," he said in a subdued tone.

"Hi Walter," Fred said. "Are you going to come out and visit us and enjoy some of this crisp fresh air?"

"I may after I've resolved several things," Walter said. "Firstly, how is your business going?"

"It's going very well," Fred said. "I may have to hire a second person before long."

"That's marvelous," Walter said. "I'm very happy for your success. Secondly, I need some information on a Brigadier General Sean Flannigan. You may have to dig deep. Something disturbs me about him."

"I'll get right on it," Fred said.

"One other thing," Walter said. "There is a close friend of mine named General Howard Metcaff who was killed in New York today. I need to know what the connection is between General Metcaff and General Flannigan. I know some of it, but there must be something more to this."

"I'm sorry to hear about your friend," Fred said. "I'll check into both of them and let you know."

"I need you to find out what special operations or projects both of these men had been working on for the last ten or more years," said Walter.

"Now that's going to be almost impossible, Walter," Fred said hesitantly. "Because I can't get access to any Pentagon files. However, I may be able to contact some of his close friends and family and see what they know."

"This is extremely important," Walter said. "I feel General Metcaff was killed because he was either working on something classified, or was involved in something that certain people wanted – badly. I'll be at my home in three hours and you can reach me there. Thank you Fred," And he hung up.

Chapter

22

Fred was also a law school graduate with an MBA from the Wharton School of Business. Well before he graduated, some of the *Big Ten* accounting firms had already courted him. He decided to go to work for the company that paid off all of his student loans.

Five years ago, Fred was working as a consultant to a major litigation law firm, performing forensic analysis on a company that appeared to be hiding assets through multiple shell companies and offshore corporations. They wanted to water down the stock to drive the price down and then purchase enough back in order to have fifty-one percent or majority ownership of the company.

He got himself into trouble when the company he first worked for set up what amounted to a Ponzi scheme to create nonexistent revenue and hide profits. Unfortunately, the three executives who concocted the scheme had been secretly wire-transferring millions of dollars to a bank in the Cayman Islands, and before Fred knew it, they just didn't show up for work anymore.

Fred was the only one left, and since he was the CFO, they assumed he knew all about it, and he ended up taking the fall. Walter heard about the case and knew some of the principals. He hired the finest lawyer for Fred's defense, and luckily, Fred was acquitted on a technicality. After the trial, Fred wanted to get even, and he knew the only way to hurt them – was in their wallets. In addition, he felt he owed the good people that worked at the company who had lost their life savings.

He went after them with a passion and within a week, working night and day, had traced the money back to a bank in the Netherlands. He had one of his friends, a whiz computer hacker, tap into and transfer all the money to a bank in Lichtenstein. They now no longer had any money to spend or pay their own bills. A note was anonymously sent to the hotel indicating what they had done. With no money, they were flown back to the U.S., where the U.S. Marshals were eagerly waiting for them.

❖   ❖   ❖

In the coming years, he worked with Leonard Schultz, Walter's lawyer, and COO, performing numerous very detailed forensic analyses for some of the companies that Walter had purchased. Fred was able to save Walter a lot of money and, in return, was handsomely paid for his research and conclusions. From that point on, Walter found another specialist to add to his arsenal of professionals.

Several years ago, he opened his own business in Fort Collins and had been doing very well ever since. Along the way, he met a woman who shared his same values and started a relationship with Danielle Smith. Danielle and Fred had been dating each other for the past several years. He had almost proposed to her on several occasions, but each time he was embroiled in a massive research project for Walter or one of his newer clients.

One particular day, Danielle walked into Fred's office and bluntly said, "When are you going to make time for me?" she asked.

"I'm sorry Danielle, I can't just stop working," Fred tried to explain to her.

"You're *always* busy!" she said. "Why don't you hire somebody for some of those smaller jobs?"

"That's a great idea." Fred thought about it and said, "I'll do that."

Danielle happened to be the sister to Don Smith, who was Rick's Foreman at the Monarch ranch.

❖   ❖   ❖

Soon after that, Fred did hire an individual, named Evan Singleton. Soon, he hired a second individual named Martha Honeycutt. Once he felt comfortable and all were on board with how he liked to do things, he invited Danielle on a short vacation to Carmel, California.

"You're kidding," she beamed with excitement. "We are going to have such a great time."

"I know we will sweetheart," Fred said. "You know, I just realized that I haven't had any kind of vacation for over five years."

Chapter

23

Duncan looked into his rear view mirror at Walter and saw that the death of General Metcaff had really affected him.

"Let's stop by Jacques new restaurant," Walter said.

"We're on our way," Duncan happily said.

"I haven't seen him since he opened his new restaurant," Walter said. "I'm told it's going to be very nice."

I hope this cheers him up a little bit, Duncan thought.

❖ ❖ ❖

Jacques Béarnaise was actually born Reginald Sparling. However, as soon as he started going to cooking school, he legally changed his name to Jacques Béarnaise. He felt that his name had to project a certain polish to his craft. He graduated from college and felt he had learned all he could, and figured it was time to apply this knowledge. He knew from the start that in order to be successful, you must always dress the part. He quickly made inroads into some of the finest hotels on the East Coast and finally got the attention of someone who appreciated his talents.

Jacques watched his mother cook and bake, and was always fascinated by the things she could make, and all without a cookbook. That's when he figured out what he wanted to be in life. He started out as a *sous-chef* in a small restaurant. Several months later he had an opportunity to go to Paris and watch Pierre Dubois, a noted five-star Michelin Chef create his masterpieces. After just a year, he returned to New York.

He had a dream to be a world-class chef. However, as luck would have it, he was drafted into the U.S. Army. While he was stationed at Fort Dix in New Jersey, he volunteered for KP duty once, just to see how the mess Sergeant was cooking for the troops. He found out it was very bland, and no one would listen to any of his ideas, so he never volunteered for KP duty again. As fortune would have it, they sent him to Fort Bliss, Texas where he finished his tour of duty in Company C, 3rd Battalion. When he got out of the Army, he went to work at a small restaurant called *The Island Hopper* in El Paso, Texas. They tried everything to grow the business, but because of the economy at the time, they were almost doomed. They were struggling to make ends meet.

One day, the owner asked Jacques, "What do you think about creating a completely new menu?"

"When I was learning to be a chef in Paris," said Jacques, beaming, "they taught me how to make several very popular French dishes. They are easy and inexpensive to prepare, and I could teach the other cooks the techniques."

"Well, we have nothing to lose," said the owner happily, as he threw up his hands. "Let's give it a try."

Within a month, they made some simple changes to convert the restaurant from hamburgers, French fries, and sandwiches, to a new French-style Bistro with only about ten menu items. Soon, the new owners were in the *black*, and they had to take reservations, because they could no longer accept just street traffic.

Jacques continued his education and went on to the International Culinary Center in New York for two years. He learned how to prepare almost every type of meat, vegetable, and salad dishes. The second year, he devoted to creating specialty pastries. He also spent time understanding the business side of how to manage a restaurant. His long-term goal was to one day make this a five-star Michelin rated restaurant.

After eighteen months, Jacques was lucky enough to land a job at one of the five-star hotels in New York. He worked there for over six years and ended up as the head chef. He didn't especially like it, after a while, because he didn't have exclusivity to design the menu that he had wanted to create.

Chapter

24

General Howard Metcaff was a Colonel at the time, working at the Pentagon for Foreign Affairs in Africa. He and his friend, Colonel Sean Flannigan, now a Lieutenant General, were on a special assignment to tie up loose ends that Hitler's Army left in the wake of their withdrawal. Every time he saw General Flannigan, he tried to avoid him, because he didn't want anything to do with him anymore.

❖   ❖   ❖

Howard was an average student in high school, and went on to college, on a football scholarship. He joined the ROTC simply as a lark, and found that he actually liked it. He excelled in all categories and his company commander recommended him to be accepted to West Point. Life there was a little more difficult than he had anticipated, but he stuck it out, and graduated as a second Lieutenant. His last year at the Point, he met Sean Flannigan, who graduated at the same time. They became great friends. Sean's father was very influential in Washington and made life simple for Sean. Howard tagged along for the ride, because at the time he had no great ambition for himself.

Whenever Sean was promoted to a new Officer rank, they also promoted Howard as well. As a result, both coasted through the U.S. Army as if they were on a company paid vacation. However, Sean's father had passed away, and he was no longer able to pull the strings necessary to keep Sean out of harm's way.

Their last duty assignment, in Northern Africa, is where they were told about a special jewel encrusted crown given to a Pharaoh's Princess. They both struggled to find out about various papyrus scrolls, and the lost pyramid, but eventually Howard had enough of the partying.

As soon as they both reached the rank of Colonel, Howard started getting serious about his position in the US Army. He tried to turn his life around and be the soldier he wanted to be when he went to ROTC and later to West Point.

❖　❖　❖

There was an electronics show hosted by the US Army and Howard was put in charge of putting it together. Walter

Donleavy was invited through Ernie's contacts in the Pentagon. That's when Walter met Howard.

"Mr. Donleavy, it's a pleasure to meet you," said General Metcaff. "What brings you here to our show?"

"A close friend of mine, General Mathew Wielding," Walter said, "He thought I might like to see the latest and greatest the Military has to offer. He is now Senator Wielding. I assume you're familiar with him?"

"Yes, of course, I am," said General Metcaff. "Let me know if I can be of any service to you."

"Rest assured, I will contact you, General," Walter said as they shook hands and parted.

❖   ❖   ❖

Over the years, Walter stayed in contact with Howard. They had dinners together at Walter's restaurants. Walter wanted a friend in the Military and working at the Pentagon was special. Walter was one of the chief reasons that Howard started to focus on his military career.

Chapter

25

Duncan drove up to Jacques' Bistro. From the outside, it looked like a typical Parisian Bistro. Right out of Paris, most of the décor was red with dark trim. As they went inside, Jacques came over to greet Walter and Duncan.

"Hello Mr. Donleavy," Jacques said happily. "I am so glad you're here. What do you think of the place?"

"It looks marvelous. Exciting and regal at the same time," Walter said.

"Why thank you Mr. Donleavy," Jacques said. "Can you stay for lunch?"

"Only if you can make my favorite dish – Trout Almandine for two?" Walter asked.

"No problem," Jacques said happily. "I will see to it personally."

"What do you think of this place Duncan?" Walter asked.

"I like it, but I'm afraid I'm more of a steak and potato man, "Duncan said.

"You have to broaden your horizons," Walter said. "After all part of your personal growth is to try new things."

Lunch arrived and the plates were put in front of Walter and Duncan.

"Oh my, Jacques," Walter said. "This looks splendid."

"Thank you Mr. Donleavy," Jacques said. "Bon appetite."

❖ ❖ ❖

After they had lunch, Duncan drove Walter home in silence. While he was driving, he would occasionally look in his rear view mirror at Walter. He looked frustrated, but at the same time, he seemed to have resigned himself to the fact that his friend was gone. *I feel helpless that I can't do something for him*, Duncan thought.

❖ ❖ ❖

Duncan Houston was born in Calimesa, California. He was an average student in high school. After he graduated, he decided to join the Marines, like so many of his classmates. He did his boot camp training at Camp Pendleton, California, where he found that he had a knack for firearms and knew this was his true calling. He also worked out and was at one time a participant in the Mr. Universe contest. One morning after roll call, his platoon sergeant asked to see him in his office.

"Private Houston," barked his Sergeant, "How would you like to go to Maryland for specialist firearm training?"

"I'd like that very much sir," said Duncan, grinning from ear to ear.

"Don't call me Sir...I work for a living," growled the Sergeant.

"When do I leave?" asked Duncan.

"You're leaving tomorrow morning at 0600," said his sergeant. "Go pack your gear son, and don't make me regret this. Now get outta here!" As he handed Duncan the new orders.

❖ ❖ ❖

The next day Duncan was on a plane out of San Diego, California, to Aberdeen, Maryland. He didn't know it at the time, but the year he would spend there, would change his life forever. He later also volunteered for a tour of duty in Vietnam. After serving two tours of duty, they transferred him, and he became one of the instructors in Vilsec, Germany, to teach NATO officers about the various weapons in the U.S. arsenal. That was where he met Steve.

Always looking for a little excitement, Duncan also trained to be a Seal for the U.S. Navy and was involved in several high-level black-ops missions that were still considered classified. He is six-foot-two and very muscular, but also agile. He sported a simple gray mustache, and had short-cropped gray hair. After his last assignment on Grenada, the missions didn't seem to provide that same adrenalin rush anymore. It seemed like just another job. He took that as a sign and decided to retire from the service after twelve years.

❖   ❖   ❖

His parents, Conrad and Martha, had come to the United States from Stockholm, Sweden in the late fifties for a better life for the family. They're original last name was actually Hakarson. The reason they changed it was that many people were having a hard time pronouncing it and bills would always misspell their last names. He had one sister named Hannah, who was an Assistant District Attorney in Riverside, California. He also had an older brother named Andreessen, who was a professional racecar driver. He was killed one day when he got too close to the outer wall.

❖   ❖   ❖

With his unique schedule with Walter, he didn't spend much time with his parents and his sister. The holidays were always difficult for him, because his brother Andreessen was killed on December 25.

Chapter

26

Rick, Liz and Frank were all flying to Billings, Montana to see how the new meat processing plant was progressing.

"I'm looking forward to seeing the new plant and our visit with Dwight," Rick said. "That was a great move to give him more control on the layout of the building. The spur line behind the Monarch Ranch plant is working out perfectly."

"I agree, Rick," said Frank. "However, I think spending time up there, and helping him through the process was a great idea. He's a natural to manage our business interests up here."

"Even though the plant is not 100% finished, he has been supplying beef and pork to most of my restaurants," Liz said. "I'm so glad I took on this project. I feel a real sense of accomplishment. Much more than when I was teaching and lecturing."

"Frank. Based on your trip up here last month," Rick asked, "Do you think Dwight is still up to our expectations? I remember when we first talked to him, he seemed like he just won the lottery."

"My feeling is that he has *exceeded* our expectations," Frank said with enthusiasm. "In fact we need to force him to take a little time off, or he'll burn himself out."

❖ ❖ ❖

Towards the back of the plane, two passengers were observing people in the first class seating area.

"I want to get this over with," said Belinda sounding irritated.

"Don't be so impatient," said Nansie.

"Easy for you to say. You have a boyfriend," said Belinda. "If Apollo found out, you'd be gone. You know her rules."

"Look, we need to stay focused," said Nansie. "By tomorrow evening, we'll be on our way back home to Paris and partying again."

❖ ❖ ❖

"I don't know about you guys," Rick said. "But ever since we left Fort Collins…..I've felt like we're being watched and followed. I might be getting apprehensive because things are going so well. I think I'll take a walk around the plane. Be right back."

Rick got up and casually walked up the left side of the plane and went into the lavatory. He stayed there for a few minutes, came out, and walked back down on the right side of the plane. He paused for a few seconds when he saw two stylishly dressed women reading a French magazine. He wasn't sure, but they seemed out of place. Rick casually walked back to his seat.

"I'm not sure, but I think we have two people following us," Rick said.

"Do you really think so?" Liz asked surprised.

"It may be a chance occurrence," Rick said. "But there are two women in the back reading a French magazine. When we depart, let's watch and see what they do."

Frank was listening, trying to make sense out of all of this. "What are you going to do if they followed us?"

"I don't know yet," Rick said. "But we'll see when we get off the plane."

❖   ❖   ❖

Rick, Liz and Frank got off the plane at Logan International Airport in Billings, Montana.

"I'll get the car…be right back," Rick said calmly.

Rick didn't go directly to the car rental agency, but went back into the airport terminal through a side door. He wanted to observe the two women whom he saw earlier. They stood at the top of the cement steps pointing in the direction of where Liz and Frank were standing. Even though they were both dressed stylishly, they had no purse or bags. They were talking and gesturing to each other, but Rick couldn't quite hear what they were saying.

Rick saw one of the two women going in the direction of the car rental area. He took that opportunity to follow her and see what he could find out. He followed her, but was out of sight from the other girl.

He got close enough to her and asked bluntly, "Why are you following us?"

"We are not following you," she said aloud. "If you don't leave me alone I'll scream for the police."

Rick grabbed her and put his hand over her mouth to stop her from screaming. But, he underestimated her and she elbowed him in his side, which temporarily reduced his hold on her. However, he quickly regained his hold of her and this time a quick chop to the neck stopped her from flailing. He was still hidden from the group, when he slapped her lightly to wake her up. At the same time, he noticed that her passport and return ticket to Paris fell out of her pocket. He also found a gun when he searched her, like none he'd ever seen before. He took it and put in his pocket.

"Why are you following us?" he said angrily.

"I don't know what you are talking about!" she said as she started to scream.

He quickly put his hand on her throat to stop her. She was now wild-eyed, because she'd been caught.

"This is a warning to go find someone else to follow," said Rick "We keep running into people with French passports following us,"

Rick *clipped* her one more time and she went limp. He picked her up, sat her down on a bench, still out of sight of the others, and went to get the car. He took her French passport, plane ticket, cell phone, and gun with him. Then he went over to get the car to pick up Liz and Frank.

"What took you so long to get the car?" asked Liz.

"Get in and I'll tell you later," Rick said. "I got this from one of the two woman that's been following us."

"It's a French passport!" Liz exclaimed, "And a neat gun and so light weight. This is odd. What's going on here?"

"I don't know, but we're going to get to the bottom of this quickly," Rick said.

❖ ❖ ❖

About an hour later as Belinda came wandering towards Nansie, rubbing her jaw.

"What happened to you," asked Nansie.

"The fellow Rick came up behind me and took my things," Belinda said.

"We have to contact Apollo about this," Nansie said. "She's not going to be happy about the fact that we've been found out."

"I also thought this was going to be an easy hit," Belinda said. "Now, I'm afraid, it's personal."

❖ ❖ ❖

As they were driving to the Monarch Meat Processing plant in Billings, Rick said, "I have a feeling we haven't seen the last of them."

"Why do you say that?" asked Frank.

"Because they only had a cell phone and a one-way ticket back to Paris," Rick said. "Also, they didn't seem to carry a purse or any bags for additional clothes."

"I wonder what they were actually after?" asked Liz. "Maybe we should let Walter know, in case he's heard about these people."

Chapter

27

Walter would never forgot the day five years ago when he told Liz, "Let me introduce you to your real mother, Hilda." Up until that time, Liz never knew Hilda was her biological mother.

Liz looked shocked and shouted out, "What! Are you kidding?"

She didn't know what to think. Her overwrought emotions took over and she was in shock. Then she turned around to look at Hilda, who had tears in the corners of her eyes. Liz got up slowly, still trying to get over the shock, and walked over to Hilda – her mother.

"If this is all true," Liz said. "I'm beside myself, but I'm also furious at the same time, that after all these years, one of my parents is still alive!"

Hilda could feel her pain and walked over to meet her, hugged her with tears running down her face, "Please don't be angry, Elizabeth," she said, "but I requested this of Walter and it was my choice. I just didn't want you to have any *baggage* to worry about as you were going to school."

❖ ❖ ❖

Rick sat bewildered by what had just happened, but was happy for Liz.

"And now, Rick, let me introduce you to your real father, Jacob," Walter said casually.

"What! This can't be!" said Rick, shocked. "Why would you do this to me?"

Rick couldn't believe what he was hearing. All this time when he drove up to Walter's estate, he was actually talking to his father as he was opening the gate.

Before Rick could say anything, Jacob told Rick, "Similar to Hilda's direction for Liz, I also didn't want you to worry but instead, be free of any possible distractions while going to school. Your mother, Isabel, passed away several years ago right here on the estate. We were both very happy and couldn't ask for anything more. Walter saw to all of our needs, and we always knew of the important things going on in your lives. We were also at both of your graduations. We quite often have dinner with Walter and reminisce about the old days. We each have our own home in the back of the estate and have pictures of you as you were growing up, so we still feel very close to you. We both feel very fortunate to have survived the war. For a long time we didn't go out in public because we were so afraid."

"We both went to night school," said Hilda, "to learn English in order to get our citizenship. We have been citizens for the last fifteen years. Please don't be angry. We made this decision years ago. But looking back, maybe we should have told you sooner."

"It's too late now," said Walter, chiming in. "I've never had a family of my own, and so I adopted all of you. As far as I'm concerned, you are all my family. This is the reason that I chose to be secretive about my business dealings. When I took on the responsibility of caring for you, Liz and Rick, I never wanted anyone to know we were a family. Someone could try to use this against your family and me."

❖ ❖ ❖

Jacob and Hilda had worked on Walter's estate for almost forty years. After each of their spouses died, they had consoled each other. Quite often they would sit out in the garden and talk about what their life would have been like if there had never been the war. However, after a while that didn't console them anymore. They realized they needed to move on and be happy that they had received a second chance at life. It took about ten years for them to start feeling better.

Jacob Teaubel, who was Walter's gatekeeper and responsible for all landscaping on the estate had been with Walter for over forty years. In addition, he had been an invaluable resource to manage his property and be a close friend when needed.

❖ ❖ ❖

Unbeknownst to anyone, Jacob and Hilda had been seeing each other for the last year or so and were going to tell Walter that they would like to get married. They weren't sure how he would react. At one time, they knew he also wanted to move to a new home, because he had promised Liz and Rick his house.

❖   ❖   ❖

Several years later, both Liz and Rick were staying at Walter's house.

"We have something to tell you, Rick," Jacob said. "However, we should get Hilda, Liz and Walter together."

"Is everything okay?" asked Rick, sounding alarmed.

"Everything is better than okay," Jacob said grinning, as they walked back into the house and motioned for everyone to meet them in Walter's study.

"We have something to tell you that affects all of us here," Jacob said. "Hilda and I have been seeing each other and are planning to get married."

"Wow, now that is great news!" Liz said eagerly, and Rick chimed in with his approval.

28

Rick, Liz and Frank drove over to the Monarch Ranch Meat processing plant close to the first Three Forks Restaurant and Lodge in Billings, Montana. As they walked in the plant, they were met by a receptionist.

"Can I help you?" she asked.

"Yes, we're here to see Dwight Robinson," Rick said.

"Let me get him for you," she said cheerfully. "And who should I say is calling?"

"Rick Benedict," he said.

A few minutes later, Dwight came through the double doors, grinning and wearing a white smock with streaks of blood on it and a white hardhat.

"Hello Mr. Benedict, and Mr. Richter," said Dwight beaming. "I'm not sure I've met this young lady though."

"This is my wife, Liz Benedict," Rick said. "She manages all of the Three Forks Restaurant and Lodge business. I thought I would introduce her to you, since she's been buying most of the meat from your operation."

"It is my pleasure to meet you," Dwight said excitedly and coming forward to shake her hand. "Come out back and I'll show you around."

Everything was spotless except where the workers were cutting up the various meats.

"By the end of the month," Dwight said, "we should be one-hundred percent ready to not only support all of the Three Forks Restaurant and Lodges and the two casinos, but also any new business you might get."

"That's great news, Dwight," said Frank enthusiastically. "Any problems we should know about?"

"Why no," Dwight said, nervous that he had missed something. "Have you heard of any?"

"No, just a question," Frank said, reassuring him. "It looks like you're in great shape."

They continued walking around the various departments in the plant to get an idea how the operation flowed. Rick did notice that this new plant was set up a little differently from the one at the Monarch Ranch.

"Can you join us for dinner tonight?" asked Rick.

"Why of course," Dwight said, beaming with pride. "I assume it will be at The Three Forks Restaurant?"

"Where else?" Liz chimed in with a small laugh. "We'll see you at 7:00 tonight," and they left the operation.

As Rick drove them all over to the Three Forks Lodge to check in, Rick remarked, "You're right, Frank. Dwight does look a little stressed. Maybe I should have a talk with him either later tonight or in the morning."

"I think that's a good idea," Frank said. "I know from where I sit, he has accomplished a lot in the short time he's been here."

"You have also helped him," Rick said. "By being up here weeks at a time to support him. All of this has created a success story, for all of us, which you can be proud of."

Frank blushed a little, at the remark.

❖ ❖ ❖

The next morning Rick met with Dwight in the coffee shop.

"Good morning Dwight. Please sit down," Rick said. "I'd like to talk to you…..about you."

Dwight tensed up, fearing the worst.

"Relax Dwight," said Rick grinning. "We *all* feel you've done a great job here."

"Whew," Dwight said. "I thought I did something wrong."

"No…not at all," Rick said. "It's just an observation. I know you want to make sure everything is working as we had planned. However, you also have to take time out for some *Dwight time*. What that means is that while you are very driven, you also need to take time out to enjoy yourself."

"Thank you, Mr. Benedict," Dwight said happily. "It's interesting that you should say that. I have actually met someone and she happens to work at the Three Forks Restaurant."

"That's wonderful!" exclaimed Rick. "I'm glad to hear that. I'll pass this along to Frank and Liz."

"I just want you to know that you have given me an opportunity that I could never have had where I grew up," Dwight said. "As you know, I think my family probably was killed in the war, but I never went back to see if any of them escaped. I want to remember them in all the good times, before the war."

"I'm sorry to hear that Dwight," Rick said. "You know that Dianna, our housekeeper was also from Croatia."

"Yes I know," Dwight said. "When she found out where I was from, we talked one evening for a long time. The war has destroyed many lives. It made me work just that much harder at my job."

"Well, again, we are all very happy how you've risen to the challenge," Rick said. "However, if you ever want to take some time off and go back to your home town, by all means, take the time."

"Thank you," Dwight said. "But for now it is still hard for me, plus I still have much work to do with the operation."

They talked a little more about the ranch and Dwight's future. Rick finally got up, which was a signal that the meeting is concluded.

"Well again Dwight," Rick said. "The place looks great and we are all very happy how you've risen to the occasion." They shook hands and left.

Rick walked back to where Liz and Frank were sitting.

"Well I spoke to Dwight," Rick said. "He's met someone. So, I don't think we have to worry about him."

"I'm happy for him," smiled Liz.

Chapter

29

Dwight was not his real name – It was Boris Bajonka. He came from a long line of butchers, and originally emigrated from Croatia. In those days, multiple generations lived on the family farm, and it was in the father's best interest to have many children. The boys were to help with the chores on the farm, and the girls were expected to marry and bring other men into the family. In either case, when one of the children got married, his parents just added another one or two rooms onto their existing house. Unfortunately, it didn't *always* work out that way, because some of the men had different aspirations. One of the key things that all men had to learn while living at the house was how to butcher cows, pigs, and sheep. This included how to make the right cuts, smoke and cure some of the meats, and make sausages.

Like most families in Europe, the war came and broke up many families and their traditional way of life. Boris, who was only fifteen at the time, was separated from his brothers and assigned as a butcher to a military unit. As the war was winding down, one day he just started walking, and left the area.... and never looked back. He headed in the direction of his home, eating when he could, which was not often enough. As soon as he was within sight of the farm, he stopped in his tracks. The farm, as he remembered it, was gone – still smoldering from a fire. He sat down and tried to cry, but couldn't.....he was too tired, hungry and angry. He made up his mind at that point to try to get as far away from that place as possible, and try to start a new life.

He traveled alone through the dead of night. Fortunately, it was summertime, but he nonetheless had to hurry to get to his final destination, because the coming winter would be harsh. He made it to Genoa, Italy and worked on the docks for a while. One day he slipped on board a ship bound for San Francisco. Within two days, he was caught stealing food and was promptly put into service in the kitchen. He now ate well, but still kept to himself. As soon as the ship got within a hundred feet of docking in San Francisco, he quietly jumped overboard. Even though the water was very cold, he swam the rest of the way to an isolated area of the coast. He eventually ended up in the Central Coast of California, working at various meat-processing plants.

Boris changed his name to Dwight Robinson to try to blend in better. He was almost six feet tall and had strong arms and shoulders from carrying half-dressed cows on his shoulders. He had dark deep-set eyes, dark curly hair, and a small mustache. He did his job well, so no one ever questioned where he'd developed his skills as a butcher. He found someone who could get him a driver's license. However, as soon as any slight problem arose, he just quietly left. Dwight never went back to his own country to see if anybody from his family was still alive. He was often homesick, but he learned to live with it. Landing a job at the Monarch Ranch was a dream come true for him.

❖　❖　❖

"While we're here, let's stop in and see Chief Running Buffalo," Liz said.

"I was thinking the same thing," Frank said.

"That's a good idea," Rick said. "I don't think we've met with him for some time now. I know we talk on the phone, but that's not enough. Let's take a run over there."

Chapter

30

Walter was sitting in his office and watching the sun slowly disappear over the hill.

He called Duncan, "Duncan have you eaten dinner yet?"

"No I have not," He said curiously. "Why do you ask?"

"I haven't been to *The Matterhorn*, my other restaurant in Manhattan in a while," Walter said. "Let's go and have a night on the town. Meet me out front in a half hour."

"Will do," Duncan said cheerfully.

As they were driving, Walter said to Duncan, "You wanted to know a little more about me. Did I ever tell you how I got to be a painter of old masters?"

"No you have not," he said, feeling ecstatic that he would share more of his life.

"It all started after I jumped off the train when I was on my way to Moscow, with Colonel Baryshnikov," Walter said. "I walked and stole rides on trains, and finally ended up in Florence,

Italy, where I spent some time just looking at art galleries for my type of paintings and found none. It was getting late, the sun was starting to set, and as I crossed the Ponte Vecchio Bridge on the Arno River, I saw the little shops selling their gold and silver jewelry. A small shop at the end of the bridge caught my eye. He was selling what looked like paintings of the old masters. I curiously went in and introduced myself to the artist, Federico Benito Mariano."

"Do you know who he was?" asked Duncan.

"No. It was a pure accident," Walter said. "Federico was a large man with a huge unkempt, straggly gray beard. He sported a very large purple fedora hat with a long white plume. He almost looked like a pirate in his outfit. He said that he liked how elegant some of the Three Musketeers looked with their huge hat and plumes, and so that was his trademark look."

"That must have been a sight," Duncan said.

"We started talking and learned Federico was an artist," said Walter, "but of a different nature. Since he was just closing his store, he invited me to have a drink with him. It was getting late and I hadn't anything special to do, so I said yes. We went to his favorite restaurant called the L'Enoteca Fuori Porta, which was just outside of Porta San Niccoló on the road up to San Miniato. As he opened the door and walked in, they all greeted him like a long lost son. We had a bottle of wine with cheese and bread and relaxed. After a while, as I was considering leaving, he told me that he had something that he thought I would be very interested in seeing."

"What was that?" Duncan asked.

"He was interesting to listen to," Walter said, "and he had a genuine quality about him, and so I trusted him. After another bottle of *Sagrantino di Montefalco,* he asked me if I wanted to see his collection of paintings. I was getting tired and had no place to sleep for the night and thought ......why not, it could be interesting, so I agreed to go with him. We walked through the winding streets, that centuries ago were alive with Roman soldiers that came through the town square called Ave del Norte Plaza. It had a grand fountain with horses and dolphins that seemed to have an endless supply of water. Remember, this all happened thirty-five years ago."

"I think it's interesting that you can remember so much, and with such clarity," Duncan said astounded.

"The outside of Federico's home," Walter continued, "appeared to be a very plain, nondescript looking building. However, when we got closer I noticed the single colossal oak, very weatherworn door with massive and very ornate hinges. There didn't appear to be any lock, but as we got closer, I saw two very small holes on the door, just above the massive handles. I watched Federico took off his Fedora, pull out a special wire from the inside of his hat lining, and insert the wire in a special sequence, and the door opened and went in."

"I'll bet it was a treasure trove of artwork," Duncan said hanging on to every word.

"While we were eating, I finally confessed to Federico," Walter said, "that I had spent ten years with both Anton Viderchia and Carlo Stavros, who taught me the fine art of oil painting. When I mentioned their names, his large bushy eyebrows jumped up. He was elated because he knew them both."

"You were very lucky," he told me, "because they rarely take on new students.

"I said that I learned a great deal from them because they were considered two of the very best artists for *old world* paintings," Walter said.

"So that's where you learned to paint," Duncan said.

"My world of painting came in two parts," Walter said. "The first part of not only painting, but recreating paintings created by the masters themselves, like Degas, Van Gogh, Rembrandt, Rubens, da Vinci, Raphael, and Michelangelo."

"Wow, you're kidding me," Duncan said in amazement.

"Finally Federico hit me with a bombshell, Walter said."

"I'm old…. and I am dying," said Federico, "and I don't have anyone to leave my artwork too. I want to pass on my secrets to you. It would be a shame to let it die with me."

"The secret he wanted to share with me was that he had mastered the art of creating counterfeit paintings," Walter said. "This included how to create an *old* canvas. At first, I was leery that he would even confide in me, since I had only known him less than twenty-four hours. However, even though it might sound morose, I was very excited because this was the second part or the next level I was looking for. Thinking back, I was only looking out for myself, because I was so excited that he would even consider me."

"So he taught you how to create counterfeit old masters?" Duncan asked.

"Yes he did," Walter said happily. "Over the next several months Federico taught me everything that I needed to know in order to create a perfect counterfeit painting, including the colors, the canvas and of course the signature of the artist. This also included the secret of how to *age* the paint, how to collect and mix certain colors, and how to find and create *old* paintings by painting on top of *old* canvases. I also learned how to duplicate the process in order to *create* old canvases."

"My goodness," Duncan burst out. "Were you ever to apply this skill to anything after you came to the United States?"

"Yes I did," Walter said, "But that's another long story. Let's eat. It'll be midnight before we get home. By the way, how do you like this restaurant?"

"It's beautiful and I noticed it's packed and it's eleven o'clock," Duncan noticed.

"This restaurant in this part of time only comes alive after nine o'clock," Walter said. "There are Broadway show patrons galore that come here to enjoy themselves," Walter said. "Let me introduce you to Jeremy Willingham, my maître de and General Manager," as he gestured to him to come over.

"Good evening Mr. Donleavy," said Jeremy. "It is so good to see you again."

"This is Duncan, my new security," Walter said.

"Hello and how are you. Did you like dinner this evening?" asked Jeremy.

"It was fantastic!" Duncan exclaimed. "Where did you get the trout for this dinner?"

"Why from Mr. Donleavy's trout farm on his estate," Jeremy said.

"Thanks Jeremy," Walter said, and watched him mingle with some of the movie stars in the crowd. "Let's go home Duncan."

Chapter

31

They drove over to *The Red Tomahawk Casino.* Workers were putting some final touches on the landscaping, when they parked their car. As they walked in, they heard the slot machines making *winner* and coins clinking sounds. They walked through the main casino towards the elevator and were on their way to the executive floor. They were met by two very large men as they punched the *open* button of the elevator.

"What is your business here?" one of the guards asked, as he brandished an automatic rifle across his chest.

"My name is Rick Benedict," he said. "We'd like to see Chief Running Buffalo, and no he's not expecting us."

The guard called the Chief's executive Secretary and told her who was here visiting the Chief.

"Yes, by all means, let them come up," she said happily.

As they rode the elevator, Frank couldn't help but notice all the special arrowheads encased in Plexiglas picture frame against one wall. The door opened and they were met by two additional guards who told them to walk through the metal detectors. At the same time, the Chief came out of his office to greet them.

"Hello, my friends," said the Chief, pleased. "It is so good to see a friendly face," as he gave Liz a big hug.

"It's good to see you too, Chief," Rick said. "We were just in town checking out our meat processing plant and thought we should stop by and see you."

"By the way, Chief, that is a fantastic display of arrowheads on your elevator wall," Frank said.

"Oh that," said the Chief. "I had that made up in in Mexico. They're all plastic, but so lifelike, don't you think? Well, come right in and have a seat."

❖   ❖   ❖

The Chief was wearing a tan colored double-breasted sport coat, a light yellow shirt with french cuffs, and dark blue slacks. They all noticed his famous casino logo on his cuff links. Rick noticed he had gotten rid of his grey double pigtails for a new more modern haircut.

"Chief, I just have to say that you look great!" exclaimed Liz.

"Thanks," said the Chief. "It was recommended that I now have to look like a twenty-first century businessman. However, when I'm in my office I still wear my moccasins and argyle socks." He lifted his leg up onto his desk.

They all had a good laugh about it.

"How is Walter doing these days?" asked the Chief.

"He's doing fine," Rick said. "We're actually on our way to see him tomorrow,"

They chatted a little longer, when the Chief said, "Would you like to be my guest for dinner tonight? Jacques has taught my people well. People come for miles around to have some corn chile with onions and grated cheese."

"That sounds great," Liz said, and they got up from their chairs.

"Tell you what. Go downstairs and do a little gambling on the house," The Chief said. "Then come back up here around eight o'clock and we'll have dinner in my private dining room. We'll have the chef make up my favorite. Imported fried armadillo snout, porcupine burgers and rabbit stew, with day old squirrel for some zest. Just kidding, I have a regular menu you can choose from."

"Okay, we'll see you later," Rick laughed as they got into the elevator.

"He's very chipper," remarked Frank, "For someone who runs two casinos that looks like they're equal to some of the Las Vegas casinos."

"Don't let any of that fool you," Liz said. "He's a hard businessman and very careful who he calls his friends."

❖   ❖   ❖

Two days later, they flew to Providence for a special meeting with Walter and Leonard. As Rick did before, he took his walk around the plane, but this time he saw nothing to give him concern.

"Looks like we're good to go," remarked Rick.

"Well, that's a good thing," Liz said.

Chapter

32

They were all sitting at Walter's conference table in his library when Leonard Schultz came in walked over to Walter and shook his hand.

"Hello everyone," Leonard said beaming. "Walter, I like what you did to the place,"

"Everything is the same," Walter said perplexed by the comment. "I only added the white board."

"That's what I meant," Leonard was smiling, trying to break the ice.

Everyone introduced himself or herself to Leonard.

"Would anyone like some coffee or tea?" Hilda asked as she peeked into the library.

"Yes, that would be great," Walter, said. "Also, we will go out to dinner at my restaurant The Alpinhoff when we break for this evening."

Frank took the time to look around the expansive looking two-story library. He marveled at the oak paneling, the oversized doors sliding into each side of the wall and the bookcases with leaded glass doors. The five monitors and computers sitting behind Walter's desk also caught his eye. *He seems to have everything readily available,* Frank thought.

❖ ❖ ❖

Most of the executives of the different companies Walter owned, didn't know each other or that they all belonged to the same holding company – Monarch Enterprises. Walter was secretive about himself and his business, but he had one business partner – Leonard Schultz. He functioned as the COO, and gave Walter weekly reports on the financial health of his companies. Walter had recruited him from Yale.

❖ ❖ ❖

Leonard was at the top of his class and single at the time. His parents died during the Great Depression but his grandparents raised him. Leonard's parents were also German immigrants who came over to the United States in 1925. He studied international corporate tax and business law. Even though he had several very good offers from prestigious law firms in New York and Chicago, he finally decided to accept the exclusive position from Monarch Enterprises. In the coming years, Leonard became a very wealthy man with only one client – Walter Donleavy.

He stood about six foot-two, with dark blue piercing eyes and a commanding expression and voice to match. He always dressed as if he were going to take over the company they were purchasing that day.

Leonard had one son named Peter. One of his personal dreams was to have Peter take over the reins of Walter's empire when he retired. Peter, however, had other plans, and they didn't include Walter's business interests – or his father's. He wanted to be recognized as a *player* in the market. Unfortunately, he wasn't quite ready for the big leagues. Subsequently, Peter created major problems for Leonard that had an even deeper impact on Walter's business interests and relationships with his clients and friends.

Because of the problems Peter created, Leonard, feeling embarrassed, ultimately resigned and retired as COO of Walter's business empire. Leonard finally moved his family to Gstaad, Switzerland, which he used as his winter home. Shortly after that, Peter had a breakdown and Leonard's wife, fraught with all that had happened, was hospitalized. Sometime later, Peter couldn't face the fact that he had failed, and he took his own life. Leonard never got over Peter's death, and always blamed Walter.

❖　❖　❖

Frank Richter came from an average Midwestern family and was lucky enough to receive a sports scholarship in lacrosse for the first two years. He went on to excel in debating and finance. He was five-foot-six, a little stocky, with red hair, and wore thick horn-rimmed glasses. His appearance would lead you to believe he was bashful. However, he was anything but timid.

When Frank was about ten years old, he was told he was adopted, but that didn't stop him from loving his adoptive parents. He was naturally unhappy after being told that his biological parents had been killed in a car accident, but youth, and his new parents, worked quickly and helped him face the sadness. Years later, however, he found out that his biological father, Paul Mathews, was still alive. He was actually a master thief living and hiding in Europe.

Frank's father Paul was divorced from his mother while he was still very young, and so he was looking for something, far from St Louis. Frank didn't have time for a relationship at this point in his life. He became the new CFO for the Monarch Ranch, the San Lorenzo Ranch in Carrizozo, New Mexico and the St. Augustine Ranch in San Ignacio, Bolivia, the latter two bred both alpaca and llama for the wool.

❖ ❖ ❖

Leonard said, "This is what Walter and I worked out that would be beneficial to all parties from a corporation tax standpoint. It is also designed to have each of you responsible for companies that will also require you to support each other."

Leonard handed everyone a package of documents. He walked up to the white board and created three new organizational charts of the various companies that Walter, Rick and Liz were going to manage. He also created a current chart as well. Everyone studied the charts and nodded in agreement.

Rick reviewed the new business plan and smiled. "I think this will work out, don't you, Liz?"

"Yes, I agree with Rick," Liz said. "That brings up a question for me, though. With me already managing the Wagon Wheel Restaurant in Fort Collins, and the twelve Three Forks Restaurant and Lodge in four states, I'm going to need to hire a CFO to manage the financial side, plus these new companies. Rick thought that maybe you, Leonard, may know someone at the main office who might want to move to Fort Collins."

"Yes, I actually have someone in mind," Leonard said. "She is currently at the company's headquarters office in Providence, and was doing quite well. She may consider moving to Colorado. I'll let you talk to her and see if you agree it would be a good fit for you, Liz."

"Great," Liz said enthusiastically." What's her name?"

"Her name is Jennifer Billingsly," said Leonard.

"When can I meet her?" Liz asked.

"I'll take you over to the office tomorrow morning," Leonard said. "Here, by the way, is her resume."

"We have accomplished a lot today," Walter, said noticing it was gradually getting dark. "I think we should break for dinner and convene in the morning to finish this up. I'll get Duncan to bring the car around."

Walter thought the session went well as he looked at Rick and Liz, and was pleased at how they reacted to the new organizational structure. However, he was curious why Frank hadn't participated more in the discussions. Throughout Leonard's presentation, Walter was also watching and listening carefully to Frank's questions. He also watched how he reacted to Liz and Rick's comments and questions. *I think this might be a better fit than I imagined,* he thought. *However, they are all still in the honeymoon phase of managing a company.*

❖ ❖ ❖

"Well, Frank, what do you think so far?" Walter asked curiously. "After all, you are a *numbers* man and most of this should make sense to you."

"Yes it does, Mr. Donleavy," Frank answered with a smile. "However, I would like a little time to digest all of this. I'm not saying I have any problems with anything. I just want to fully understand."

"Fair enough," Walter said.

Chapter

33

Minutes later, they all got into Walter's limousine and were on their way to downtown Providence and *The Alpinhoff Restaurant.* They drove slowly down the long winding driveway, listening to the crunch of the rocks under the weight of the car. They came to a very ornate oversized heavy metal gate, which opened effortlessly. Duncan turned right onto the main road. He happened to catch a small flicker of light in his rear view mirror, just as they left the driveway. Soon headlights appeared, but at that distance, it was too far to make out the license plate. The vehicle appeared to be following them. To satisfy his curiosity, he made several right and left turns but they still followed them, at a safe distance.

❖　❖　❖

"Stay a little farther behind them," a voice said. "I think I know where they are going. Call our contact. We may have to change our approach. Have the other team meet us there."

As they drove on the dark streets, they waited for a phone call.

"Now that you've identified them and know where they're going," said the caller, "We'll have the second team at your location within the hour. In the meantime, stay out of sight and don't interfere." The caller hung up.

❖   ❖   ❖

"Mr. Donleavy, I think we have someone following us," Duncan said scanning his side view mirrors.

"I suspected that when you made several turns back there," Walter said. "Let me make a call." Walter called Ernie.

"Ernie, this is Walter. We may need your help on something."

"What can I do for you?" Ernie said.

"Duncan just spotted a car following us," Walter said. "We are on our way to The Alpinhoff for dinner."

"Let me drive over and see if I notice anything suspicious in the outer perimeter," Ernie said. "I'll give you a call when I have something."

"Thanks Ernie," Walter said and hung up.

Frank was amazed at what had just happened. *This is what's it's like to be a billionaire,* he thought?

❖   ❖   ❖

They drove up to the restaurant and parked in a special space reserved only for Walter Donleavy. As Duncan opened the door for Walter and his friends, he scanned the area to see if they were still being followed. They walked in, and were immediately escorted to Walter's private dining room. As they were being seated, Walter made sure he was sitting next to Frank Richter.

"Well, Frank. How do you like my operation so far?" asked Walter.

"Frankly, I'm a bit overwhelmed, but feel very fortunate to be a part of it," Frank said. "I think it's amazing how you've been able to assemble most of your companies to support each other's products and business interests. I do have one question, though."

"Yes what is it?" asked Walter.

"Most of your companies rely on each other for support," Frank said. "They ship them, the product they produce, so they can continue the production cycle. Isn't that a little dangerous? If for some reason one of the companies could not deliver, it could have an overall domino effect on the other companies."

"Very astute observation and somewhat correct," Walter said. "However, what these charts don't show is that each of my companies has a back-up plan. Each has the authority to find a secondary and in some cases a third source, to provide them the raw product, when and if needed."

"I thought as much," Frank said, clearly pleased.

"Frank, I have a different question for you, unrelated to this weekend," Walter said.

"Yes, what is it?" Frank asked.

"When was the last time you spoke to your father, Paul?" asked Walter casually.

This caught Frank by surprise, as he hesitated to answer. "It's been a while. Maybe a year," Frank answered. "Why do you ask?"

"I would like to contact him," Walter said.

"I'll get you his phone number when we get back to your house," Frank said, looking puzzled. *I wonder why he wants to talk to him.*

"Thank you," Walter said. "By the way, how did you like your steak?"

"It is the best steak I've ever eaten," remarked Frank appearing satisfied. "Is this from the Monarch Ranch?"

"No, this is Kolbe beef, which I breed on my estate," Walter said. "As well as the trout that Leonard and I are eating. It can't get any fresher than this."

That was another positive surprise for Frank that didn't show up on any organizational charts Leonard showed them.

Chapter

34

Ernie drove over to the restaurant and casually walked up and down the streets in the shadows of the trees and bushes, looking for anything that seemed out of place. He was innocently leaning against the side of one of the trees, across the street from the restaurant, wearing his favorite old baseball cap, tennis shoes, and an old sweatshirt that said, *Old Mississippi*. Standing across the street from the restaurant, he saw a flicker of light in a parked car as if someone was lighting a cigarette. They were about five cars back, parked on the street, looking as if they were waiting for someone. He casually strolled up the opposite side of the street and glanced over to the car. It was a small two-lane street, so he could easily hear the light chatter of women speaking French. He passed them and they took a casual glance at him, but continued their conversation.

Well this could get interesting, Ernie thought adjusting his hat. He silently came up behind them to write down the model and license plate number and, then casually walked back to his car.

About ten minutes later, a different car drove up right next to the parked car. He heard some hardly audible exchange in French. The parked car left soon and the new car took its place. They continued to watch the front of the restaurant.

Ernie called a friend of his at the Providence Police Precinct.

"Hi Bill. This is Ernie. I'm standing in front of the Alpinhoff Restaurant on Firestone Blvd. and a car just took off in a hurry. I think they might be casing the place."

Ernie gave him the make, model number and license plate number of the car. Ten minutes later and six blocks away from the restaurant, four police squad cars converged, surrounded them, and forced them to stop their car.

"This is the Police," the Officer yelled into a bullhorn. "Get out of the car.....now!

"Hey what do you want," she said. "We didn't do anything wrong?"

"We'll see about that!" said a police officer, cautiously walking up to the car with his gun drawn. "Search em boys, inside and out."

"We found two special handguns," said the other Officer, "Stuffed between the front seats. We found two more guns plus two additional ammo clips and several packs of French cigarettes, hidden under a blanket in the trunk.

"Those are not ours," she said. "We just rented this car this morning."

"Take them in boys," said the officer. "Interesting, ladies. No name on the gun – or serial number."

❖ ❖ ❖

They finished dinner and got back into Walter's limousine. Ernie alerted the Police and watched as the second car started up to follow Walter. He got into his own car and followed them keeping a block between them. Three blocks later this time, six Providence police cars, blocked their car, with sirens blaring and guns drawn.

The Police yelled through a bullhorn, "Get out of the car and show me your hands – now!"

"What is this?" the driver asked bewildered, as they slowly got out of their car.

"We have it on good authority that you're carrying concealed weapons," said the Officer. "Search the car, and especially the trunk."

"Hey will you look at this?" said the other officer. "Two more of those special guns we picked up earlier with silencers hidden in the front seats. Going hunting for something in the city?"

"Search them, so we can see who they are," the first Officer said.

"All I found was a French passport, cell phone and a return ticket to Paris," he said.

"Take em in boys," said the Sergeant.

Ernie watched from a distance and smiled. *This worked out better than I thought.*

Ernie called Walter on the phone. "There were two cars with two women in each car. The second car just was picked up by the Police as you were leaving. They were fully loaded and ready to go hunting."

"Excellent," Walter said, grinning. "I thought as much. Anything unusual about them?"

"Well, they are all women and kinda good looking," Ernie said. "And they all have French passports with a return flight to Paris on them plus a cell phone. They also had a custom built .22 caliber gun with a built in silencer, I'm told."

"That is interesting," Walter said. "Thanks for your help Ernie," and hung up the phone.

❖ ❖ ❖

Ernie drove over to the Police station, now wondering who they really were. He walked in and asked for Bill, his friend at the station.

"Hi Bill," Ernie said enthusiastically. "I thought I'd come down and see that special gun you found on them."

"Yeah, sure you did," Bill said smiling at him, as he handed him the gun.

"I've seen a lot of guns in my time," Ernie said. "But this is unique. A small caliber with a built in silencer." Ernie pulled out the magazine and noticed it was still full. Then he pulled back on the barrel and the cartridge in the chamber popped out.

"I can't seem to pull the trigger," Ernie said. That's when he noticed upon closer examination a thumb print registration to fire it. "The interesting part is that there's no manufacturer's name or serial number. Definitely, a customized gun made especially for them. There are only a couple of manufactures in the world that could provide this type of service."

"I think you're right," Bill said. "But you *do* know I can't hold them for more than twenty-four hours because they haven't actually done anything, but carry an unregistered firearm."

"That's true," Ernie said. "However, I'll bet that one of the four ladies you have locked up back there has the right fingerprint for this weapon. If you match the person to the gun, then you can charge them with having an unregistered firearm with intent to do bodily harm, and send them to jail, or you can escort them to the airport and tell them they're lucky today and ask them never to come back again. Especially since they already have their ticket back to Paris."

"I'll think about it," said Bill grinning.

I'm dreading all the paperwork that I'd have to fill out, he thought, *especially since they're foreign nationals.*

"Let me make a call to someone," Ernie said, and left. "Can you hold them for at least a day?"

"I think I can," said Bill. "What do you have in mind?"

"I'll tell you later," said Ernie, and left.

Chapter

35

Jimmy was doing well at the restaurant and he now wanted to start having a little fun. When he was in Vietnam, he played cards with friends and was considered a good card player, but in those days, they only played for nickels and dimes. Jimmy Hackensack heard about a game that sometimes celebrities would sit in and he was excited that one of his friends invited him.

"Come on in, Jimmy, and sit down," said Rocky smiling from ear to ear. "We have any type of booze you want, and plenty of food. Just ask one of the girls to get you what you want."

"Gosh thanks, Rocky," Jimmy said gushing with enthusiasm.

All the girls were topless as they constantly brought the players drinks and snacks to eat. The first time he played at his place, Rocky let him win a little to give him a *taste*. Over the course of the next several months, Jimmy started winning some, but losing more. But he also got the fever along the way. He owed too much and he always thought he could get it back. At the same time, Rocky found out a lot about Jimmy and his business and knew he could play on his weakness.

"Look, Rocky, I'm going to pay you back," said a frightened Jimmy. "I just need a little more time."

"That's fine," said Rocky. "However, I'm no charity and the going rate is fifteen percent of the unpaid balance each month. Now I know you're good for it, but maybe I should come over to your place and make sure things are working out. After all, I have a big investment to watch over."

"No, don't do that!" Jimmy shouted. "I'll get your money," and turned to walk away.

"Don't forget," Rocky said. "I always get paid."

Jimmy left the room and slammed the door behind him.

Turning back to the other players, Rocky said. "You know boys….I've always wanted to own a nightclub. It sounds like this might be the one."

"Do you really think he'll let you in as a partner, boss?" his friend asked.

"I don't see that he has any choice," said Rocky feeling triumphant. "He's a pushover."

❖ ❖ ❖

Steve had known Jimmy a long time. Through the years, their paths crossed often, and though they had never served in the same Army unit, they attended each other's classes in Vietnam and then in Korea, and had developed a unique bond. When Steve left the service, they lost touch with one another.

Jimmy was a *tunnel rat* when he was in Viet Nam. He volunteered for this duty because he was around five-foot-two, on the thin side but very wiry. He had been on at least forty missions that Steve knew of. He had always cheated death because he was extremely cautious – and lucky. His body size fooled many people….until you tangled with him. When not on duty, he could easily throw down a twelve-pack of warm beer and still hit the bull's eye playing darts from twenty-five feet away.

After leaving the service, Jimmy ended up at the VA hospital suffering from a variety of things, primarily from his duties as a *tunnel rat*. He hadn't completely recovered from his problems, but he couldn't take it anymore and left. He didn't tell anybody where he was going. His sister finally found him in a soup kitchen of the local church, living day-to-day on the streets of Sausalito, California. She helped him turn himself around, because by then both their parents had passed away and Jimmy was all that was left of their family.

❖   ❖   ❖

Rocky Cappellini finally woke the next morning with a start, still wearing his bloodied tuxedo.

"Where is everybody?" he yelled out, in a stupor. "My jaw is killing me. What happened? I got blood all over my tuxedo…. and it's a rental!"

"I'm here boss," said his driver, who was still holding an ice-pack to his groin. "I took the other guy to the hospital to get his nose fixed. He also told me to leave him and he'd get a ride home. I don't think he's coming back."

"Where's my wallet?" Rocky yelled out.

"You must have dropped it, when…...." he just let the sentence trail off.

Rocky was angry, and he knew how to take care of people who made him angry. He made a few phone calls to friends.

"Yeah, come on over right now," Rocky said.

❖　❖　❖

Steve still had Rocky's wallet, so he glanced inside to see where he lived. *I better double check on this guy*, he thought, *just to make sure he doesn't do something stupid.* It was nighttime as he drove over to the address in Rocky's wallet. As he pulled up, he saw two other cars drive up and four guys got out of the car, and he thought, *Why are there so many people picking up their dry cleaning at ten at night? I think I know why.*

❖　❖　❖

"How would you guys like to make a cool *grand*?" Rocky asked the four other men in the room.

"Yeah sure, why not?" they all chimed in. "I ain't got nothin better to do tonight."

They were all standing in the back of the store listening to Rocky. As Rocky was letting everyone know what he wanted to do, suddenly a car came crashing through the front plate glass, through all the laundry hanging all the way to the back area. Immediately behind that car was a second car crashing through the other window.

"What the hell?" Rocky shouted. "Get those guy's in the cars!"

With guns drawn, they ran over to both cars. Unfortunately, there were no drivers in either of the cars.

"There's nobody here," one person yelled.

"This one either," the other person yelled. "Hey, this is my car! Look what they did to it?"

Steve had moved the cars so they would face the storefront, started up the engine, put it in gear, with a brick on the accelerator and put the car in drive. The momentum did the rest. As he stood across the street to admire his handy work, he smiled, walked back to his car and drove off.

"Who did this?" asked one of the people.

"I can guess who it was, and this ain't over," Rocky said.

"Hey there's a note attached to the steering wheel," one of the guy's said. It says,

"If you value your life, find another line of work. I now know where each of you live and if you pursue this, go and buy your burial plot now, so it won't be a big surprise to your wives, when the police come and ask them to identify the bodies"

"Rocky! Who is this guy and what did you do to piss him off like this?" asked one of the people. "On top of that, how do I explain my messed up car to my wife?"

"Yeah, a grand isn't going to fix my car either," the other person said. "I'm outta here," and they all left.

Rocky sat down and was at a loss for words. All his *boys* had left him as he sat there wondering what he was going to do. He had never been beaten before, and who did it all without killing anybody.

Chapter

36

Ernie called Walter the next morning and said, "Walter, what do you want me to do with these so called French *assassins*?"

"We have to find out where their boss is located," Walter said. "We know it is someplace in or around Paris. I have an idea. Let me make a call. If he agrees to come with me, can we take one of them out of town? I'll call you right back."

Ernie was now curious to know what Walter was planning.

Walter made the phone call, "Terrific," he said, "I'll pick you up at your home in a few minutes." and hung up.

He then called Ernie back, "Meet us at that old deserted warehouse by the river."

"Okay. I know where it is. I'll stop at the Police station and pick up one of the girls," said Ernie, "We'll see you there," and hung up the phone.

"Hilda, have Duncan bring the car around," Walter said standing in the kitchen doorway.

Duncan was in front of the house, a few minutes later. Walter got in his car and said, "We need to pick up Aki in front of his house."

"Okay Mr. Donleavy," said Duncan, who had never met Aki and wondered why he needed him.

"Hello Aki," Walter said. "So glad you could join us."

"It is my pleasure," said Aki, as he bowed to Walter. He was also carrying a small satchel and they drove off.

In minutes, they drove through the security gates from his estate, passing Jacob, his gatekeeper, and onto the main highway. Duncan happened to look into his rear view mirror and noticed Walter speaking softly to Aki. After a half hour drive, they pulled off the main road to a secluded area by the wharf. At one time, it was a bustling factory with people assembling refrigerators. They pulled up to the old factory and got out. They walked through a heavily graffiti painted door and went upstairs to the second floor, where there was more graffiti on the walls. There were broken windows everywhere. In the middle of the floor was Ernie, with one of the women, tied to a chair with a hood over her head.

"My name is Walter Donleavy. I'm the person you and your pathetic friends have been trying to kill. I want to know who ordered this and why?"

"I'm not telling you anything!" she screamed out.

"Oh, I think you will, Alana," Walter said without hesitation. "I would like to introduce you to a very good friend of mine. He is the foremost expert on how to administer pain. He has personally practiced this technique successfully for many years. I should also add that this method was developed, and is still in practice, for over five-thousand years."

"I don't care!" Alana screamed, as they pulled the hood off her face.

She squinted with the light in front of her.

Aki walked over to her, unrolled his kit on the floor in front of her. He showed her a variety of bright and shiny surgical tools, which would normally scare anyone. He pulled out one of his acupuncture needles, and inserted it quickly into the side of her neck.

"What did you do!" she yelled. "Make him stop!"

Aki stood in front of her and said calmly, in a matter of fact voice. "In approximately thirty seconds, your right hand will go numb. When I insert the second needle into the left side of your neck, your left hand will go numb. I have now reduced the flow of oxygen to the brain and within fifteen minutes, you will pass out. In another fifteen minutes, if I don't administer the antidote – you'll be dead."

"You are all crazy!" Alana cried out. "I'll never tell you anything!"

Duncan looked on with fascination, but felt sorry for the girl at the same time.

"You don't have long to live," Walter said. "Who and where is your boss? Oh, by the way. I think I forgot to mention something else about the side effects. Five minutes before you die you will experience such excruciating pain, you'll wish for a bullet."

"You're lying!" she yelled out. "I'm still not telling you anything!"

"All right then, I guess we'll leave," Walter said. "Let's pack up and get out of here."

They walked about twenty feet away, and Alana cried out, "Wait! I can't stand the pain anymore! What do you want to know?"

"What is your boss's name?" asked Walter.

"Her name is Apollinaris Bonnaire," she said, now crying with her mascara running down her cheeks. "Take these pins out and give me the antidote."

Aki walked back to her and pulled the two pins from her neck.

"Where can I find her?" Walter asked.

"She has a small castle she calls *Chateau de Carlson*," she said, crying as tears were rolling down her cheeks. "But you'll never get to her. It's heavily fortified and not even with all your skill can you *ever* get to her." Soon after that, she started slurring her words, her head dropped forward and she passed out.

"What do you recommend we do with her?" Ernie asked. "I doubt seriously that Apollinaris is going to welcome her back into her organization, especially since she told us where to find her."

"I agree," said Walter. "Wake her up and give her a thousand dollars, her passport and put her on a train to somewhere in Oregon. At least she can still live some type of life."

"We've got to find out where this *Chateau de Carlson* is actually located," Walter said. "I think Fred might *now* be able to help with this.

"Okay, I'll take care of her and get her on a bus or train," Ernie said.

"Thanks Ernie," Walter said, as they left.

❖   ❖   ❖

Aki, Duncan and Walter drove back to his estate.

"Thank you Aki," Walter said, pleased. "You put on a great show back there."

"You're welcome, Mr. Donleavy," Aki said.

"You mean that was all a show?" Duncan said looking shocked, in the rear view mirror.

"Yes it was Duncan," Walter said smiling.

"What if she wouldn't have told you anything?" Duncan asked.

"Aki can use those pins to create the *illusion* of pain," Walter said. "Are you bothered by all of this? After all, she was planning to kill me and I'm sure she'd kill you as well, so there would be no witnesses."

"You're right, Mr. Donleavy," Duncan said. "She probably would have."

"Make no mistake of that!" Walter said assertively.

Another part of Walter's world has become known, Duncan thought. *He is one unique individual, who I actually know very little about.*

Chapter

37

That night Walter called Paul Mathews.

"Paul, this is Walter Donleavy."

"Well, hello Walter," said Paul excitedly. "Haven't talked to you in a while. How is Frank doing?"

"He's doing just fine," Walter said. "However, I have a question for you."

"What is it?" asked Paul curiously.

"Are you still familiar with the layout of the Sir William Sheffield Museum in London, England?" Walter asked

"Yes I am actually," said Paul. "Why do you ask?"

"Not over the phone," Walter said. "I'll plan on a trip to London, in a few days. I would like you to meet me at the Creighton Hotel on Mulberry Street. Can you do that?"

"Yes of course," Paul said, sounding concerned. "Is there anything I need to prepare for this meeting?"

"I don't know at this time," Walter said. "Between now and then, I'm sure I'll come up with something. By the way, how are you doing over there? Staying out of trouble, I hope?"

"Yes I am," Paul said. "I actually got a job at the Frankfurt Main train station."

"Excellent," said Walter. "I'll see you in London," and hung up the phone.

❖   ❖   ❖

Paul Mathews was now a retired cat burglar, living in Frankfurt, Germany until Walter could figure out how to get him back to the United States without being arrested. Paul left because he'd decided he couldn't handle family life. He traveled to all the hot spots in Europe to ply his trade and live that good life. He was one of the best thief's in the industry. He had been arrested numerous times, but never convicted, except for that one time in England at the Sir William Sheffield Museum.

Frank Richter was actually Paul's son. Several years ago, Frank found out his biological father was *not* killed, but still alive. When Frank found out his father was still alive, he was angry and didn't want anything to do with him. However, over time, they called each other occasionally just to see how things were going. Frank still harbored resentment towards his father. But in the back of his mind, he figured he was still his father, and while Frank had not made any effort to forgive him, he still missed him as a son growing up.

❖ ❖ ❖

The next day after everyone had left Walter called Duncan, "Duncan I would like to schedule a trip to London, England."

"Okay," Duncan said. "When would you like to leave?"

"In two days," Walter said. "We'll be gone for about three to four nights."

❖ ❖ ❖

Walter and Duncan were flying from the T. F. Green Airport to the London City Airport. As usual, Walter liked to sit in the co-pilots seat when taking off and landing.

"I told you didn't I that I'm going to buy a new plane?" Walter said casually.

"Yes, you mentioned that," answered Duncan. "When do you think that will be?"

"Very soon," Walter said. "In fact, we may stop in Wichita on our way back home and look at the Raytheon 1900 series ship. However, before I buy it, we need to build a runway and a hanger on Rick's Monarch Ranch. I've talked to the Planning Commission in Fort Collins about getting a permit to take off and land on the ranch. With a little persuasion, I think they'll come around. And lastly, we need to find a pilot for Rick at his ranch."

"I might be able to help you with that," Duncan said proudly. "I have some friends in the airline industry who might be interested."

"Excellent," Walter said. "We'll keep that in mind."

❖   ❖   ❖

They landed at London City Airport at dusk and were still able to see a little daylight. They got off their plane, went through customs, walked over to the car rental agency, and drove directly to the Creighton Hotel, which was close to Trafalgar Square.

"I just love this hotel," Walter beamed with pride. "Before the war, I used to dream about staying here."

"It's a great looking place all right," Duncan said, just happy to be in London.

They walked up to the check-in counter, took their keys and headed towards the elevator. They were escorted by a porter, dressed smartly in a grass-green uniform with gold tassels on his sleeve and shoulders. They went to Walter's room first.

"Come over and see me when you get un-packed," Walter said, as he walked into his room.

"I'll be right over Walter," Duncan said.

Duncan unpacked and strapped on his favorite weapon, a Berretta Brigadier with four clips. *I'm so grateful that James got me a license to carry a firearm internationally,* he thought. He left the room and walked two doors down to Walter's room. As he was about to knock, he noticed an individual standing against the wall by the elevator at the end of the hallway. Duncan knocked on the door and heard a shuffling of feet inside. The door opened, and he saw Walter, standing there. But he also noticed he had a visitor – holding a gun in her hand.

"Come right in and show me your hands," she said holding a gun to Walter's head.

"Mr. Donleavy….are you all right?" asked Duncan, angry that he hadn't been here.

"Yes, I'm fine," said, Walter. "She was already here, hiding in the closet when I walked in."

"What is it you want?" asked Duncan, angrily.

"I want him…..dead," she said, amused. "Throw your weapons on the floor…carefully."

"I don't think we've had the pleasure," Walter said. "Why do you want me dead?"

"I don't, but somebody else does and is willing to pay a lot of money to kill you," she answered.

"How much are you getting paid to kill me?" Walter asked.

"I might as well tell you," she replied. "It's five million dollars."

"I'll give you ten million dollars, *not* to kill me," Walter said casually. He slowly walked over to one of the chairs so he would be directly opposite of where Duncan was standing with the gunman standing between them. "Don't you think that's a fair price Duncan?"

Before Duncan could answer, and for a split second, as she looked towards Duncan for his response, he heard two little pops as she fell onto the carpet. Walter was holding his Derringer Cobra and had taken two shots. One in her chest and the other to her forehead. She had a surprised look on her face as she dropped to the carpeted floor with a thud. She never knew what hit her.

"Let's get out of here, Duncan!" Walter said.

Duncan was amazed how quick all this had happened.

"I didn't know you carried a Derringer," a stunned Duncan remarked by what he'd just witnessed.

"There is still a lot you don't know about me," Walter said wryly. "Go through her pockets. Maybe we'll get lucky and find out who she is and who sent her."

Duncan searched her and said, "All I could find is this French passport, with a return ticket to Paris, and a cell phone, plus this interesting gun. I'll take it with us."

"Suddenly, we are inundated with French speaking women that wish to do us or rather me, harm," Walter said. "Let's go, Duncan."

"But they have our passports and know our names," Duncan said.

"Generally, I never use my real name and I always use a phony passport.....you included," Walter said. "Didn't you ever wonder why I always checked us into the hotels and not you? Well, now you know. Put her in the closet where she was hiding. She'll probably be found by the maid the next day."

They went out the door and into the hallway as if nothing happened. Duncan noticed that the person at the end of the hall was no longer there. They went down the back stairs, found their car, got in and drove off.

"Let me see that French passport, Duncan," Walter said. "Her name is Bella Moreau. The address is a post office box number. Let's call Fred and see if he can shed some light on this."

"Okay, but where are we going?" asked Duncan.

"Just drive, and get us to the Paddington train station," Walter said. "I have to call Paul and see where he is right now."

Chapter

38

"By now Bella should have finished her assignment," Apollo said, impatiently. "Call her, Aurelia, and see when we can expect her!"

They called her cell phone, which Duncan had in his hand. It rang several times and Duncan looked at Walter.

"Give me the phone, Duncan," Walter said.

"Hello? Who is this?" asked Aurelia.

"I'm the person your Bella tried to kill," Walter said calmly. The phone went silent for a moment.

"This must be Walter Donleavy, or should I call you Alfred Berger," said Apollo in a cocky tone. "It seems that you are quite resilient."

"Why are you trying to kill me?" Walter asked.

"Because it pays so well," answered Apollo feeling self-confident. "You have become quite a challenge for me."

"Maybe you should consider getting into another line of work," Walter said.

"Oh….And why is that? Apollo asked.

"Because you're obviously not very good as an assassin!" Walter said and hung up.

Walter looked at Duncan, smirked and said, "She'll call back. Her ego will force her."

"That arrogant fool!" Apollo said. "Call him back!"

The phone rang again, and Walter, smiling towards Duncan answered, "Have you changed jobs yet? Don't answer that. By now, my guess is that you've been hired to kill me. Are you going to tell me who that person or persons are? By my count, at least eight of your operatives are either in jail or – dead."

The phone went dead and Walter threw the phone into the nearest trashcan.

"I guess she doesn't want to talk to me anymore," Walter re-marked, bemused by the caller.

Suddenly Walter's own phone rang and he recognized the number.

"Hello Paul. Where are you at this moment?" Walter asked.

"I'm just getting off the train at Paddington," Paul said.

"Stay where you are. We'll come pick you up at the front of the station by the curb," Walter said, and hung up.

"I just realized I now have a bigger concern," Walter said looking glum.

"What's that?" Duncan asked curiously.

"This person knows me by my current name," Walter said. "But she obviously also knows me by my real name – Alfred Berger. Very few people know that."

"What do you mean your *real* name?" Duncan asked sounding confused.

"That's another long story I'll tell you about later," Walter smiled slightly.

I guess I don't know much about Walter Donleavy or Alfred Berger, he thought. *The mystery just gets bigger.*

"The gun she was carrying is unique," Duncan said. "It's definitely custom-built, small caliber with a built-in silencer. It also has no serial number or a manufactures identification. Something like this, you would think they'd want the world to know. They sure make them small these days. The year I spent at Aberdeen in the Army, I never saw anything like this. I must admit, it is unique."

❖ ❖ ❖

As they drove over to the Paddington train station, Duncan asked, "Where did you learn to shoot like that?"

"You know of course that I've had several other security people before you," Walter said. "They all convinced me that one day they might not be close enough to protect me. Consequently, Ernie purchased this Cobra Derringer for me that I keep in my watch pocket. Today was the first time in about twenty years I've had to use it."

"I'm very happy you did," Duncan said relieved. "I saw the fire in your eyes when you pulled the trigger."

"War has a way of preparing you for just that moment," Walter said.

"There's Paul," Walter said pointing towards him, as they pulled up to the curb. "Hello Paul, please get in. This is Duncan, my security. Change of plans. We're not going to the Creighton Hotel. Duncan, take us to the Kensington Plaza."

❖　❖　❖

Apollo was sitting on her throne-like oversized chair, stewing.

"So far, nine of my team has failed!" she yelled out. "Call Ulrich for me!" she shouted.

"Here is Apollo," Aurelia said as she handed her the phone.

"Hello Ulrich," she said. "This job is turning out to be a nightmare."

"I'm surprised, Apollo," Ulrich said coughing on the phone. "You obviously didn't do your homework on him."

"He apparently has a much better security team than you've led me to believe," Apollo said. "You also never told me how you knew him as Alfred Berger!"

"One of his close associates, and I won't say who, told me in confidence," Ulrich said. "Now do your job…..or give me my money back! I'm sure I can find people more imaginative that could do the job." He hung up.

❖　❖　❖

Ulrich made a call to his client.

"Hello? Who is this?" he asked.

"It is me…Ulrich."

"Is the job done?" he asked.

"No…unfortunately," Ulrich said disappointedly. "It seems your *friend* is more resourceful than you indicated."

"I don't care for your excuses!" he barked. "Don't call me again, until the job is finished! I'm also under a tight schedule for the next phase of my own plans, so take care of this!"

Chapter

39

"I'll call Fred and see if he's found out anything on this Bella, and her French passport," Walter said.

"I don't have much," Fred said. "But it seems the passport might be a phony. The fact that you've recently run into eight or nine of these French women, tells me something. They may be part of some organization that has been trying to stay under the radar. I did however make a call to INTERPOL, to see if anything like this has surfaced. They said they really aren't sure because it's been spotty."

"It sounds like a very sophisticated group," Walter said. "Somebody is going to a lot of trouble to try and kill me. Why… I don't know."

"I'll keep searching and see if I come up with anything else," Fred said.

"Thanks Fred." And he hung up.

"Maybe Ernie can call some of his friends in France," Walter said to Duncan.

"Hi Walter," Ernie said. "Are they still hounding you?"

"Yes, regrettably. Ernie, do you have anybody you could contact in France?" Walter asked. "There is something going on here that leads me to believe there is more to this than meets the eye."

"Offhand, I can't think of anyone," Ernie said. "But let me make some calls."

"Do that, because I'm now worried not just for me, but for Liz and Rick, even others that connected to me or around me." Walter said.

"I'll let you know," Ernie said, sounding now more concerned than ever.

"One other thing, Ernie," Walter said. "It might be a coincidence, but this all started when you gave me that red leather book you got from Kirk Odorkian last year. One of the names that stood out is the name, Janus Parn. He lives in Tallin, Estonia. He was one of the inmates detained with me at Sachsenhausen Concentration camp. It may be nothing, but I'll have Fred check it out."

"That *is* a coincidence," Ernie said. "And I know you don't believe in coincidences. I'll let you know."

❖   ❖   ❖

Duncan drove them to the Kensington Plaza Hotel. As they got out of their car, they walked up a short flight of dark green marble steps. They were met by a smartly dressed porter at the top of the steps, holding the door open for them.

"Welcome to the Kensington Plaza," said the porter pleased.

Walter nodded to him and said, "Let's get something to eat," as Walter guided them to the coffee shop.

They sat, and ordered something from the menu. Walter looked around and was happy it was not crowded.

Duncan also scanned the area to see if anything seemed to stand out. Everything seemed normal.

"Paul, I have a special request for you," Walter said. "When I reviewed your background, I remembered that you are familiar with the Sir William Sheffield Museum and their underground storage area."

Interesting that he has access to that type of information, Duncan thought.

"Yes I am," said Paul blushing. "That's the only time I was ever caught, and went to Acklington prison for it," he said proudly, as if wearing a badge of honor.

Duncan was listening to all of this and getting nervous about associating with a known criminal.

"This is a long shot, and it could put you in a lot of danger," Walter said. "But I think the papyrus documents everyone has been looking for.....might still be in those crates. They are probably labeled, Dr. Benjamin Fazihd. I know it's been over forty years, and as I said, it's a long shot."

"The good thing is that there were no cameras down there at the time," Paul said. "Because nothing down there is really considered valuable."

"That makes sense," Walter said. "Are you up for the challenge?" he said, looking at Paul and waiting for a response.

"Let's do it," Paul said enthusiastically.

"You must be very careful when you rummage around down there," Walter said. "I can't imagine there would be too many boxes or crates with his name on it. That's assuming....they still have them. I will tell you this, though. There are also other people looking for those scrolls. Plus they are also very fragile, so handle them with extreme care."

"When do you want me to do this?" asked Paul.

"Tonight, if you're up for it," Walter said. "Any special tools you may need?"

"No, I don't think so," said Paul.

"We'll check into this hotel and wait for you," Walter said.

"It's now getting dark, and the perfect time to put my skills to use," Paul said, with a wink.

Duncan watched Paul leave, waited until he was out of sight, and said to Walter, "Mr. Donleavy. I think this goes way beyond me supplying security for you."

Walter looked at him with his cold blue eyes and without any hesitation said, "If you like, you can leave now right and go sit in the plane, until we have to take off. Men have died for those scrolls, including a very personal friend of mine. I aim to see that those papyrus scrolls, assuming we find them, are returned to their rightful owners....The Heliopolis Museum in Cairo, and the Government of Egypt. If this is all too much for you, then when we get back home, I'll give you a hundred thousand dollars, you'll sign a non-disclosure agreement concerning me and my business interests, and you are welcome to leave."

"Now, wait a minute," Duncan said surprised by how quickly Walter was ready to call it quits.

"As you can see with the short time you've been with me…
.I don't have a minute," Walter said in a decisive tone. "I have
spent years building my business and it's all legal. I don't have
the luxury of second-guessing my competition. As I said, if this is
all too much for you….I understand."

Duncan sat there, still stunned. He had his head down, staring at the cup of coffee in front of him. He let it all sink in, before he said anything. He knew he would have to make a choice
quickly, before he would be out of a job.

"Mr. Donleavy," Duncan said, his head still bowed down. "I
want to apologize for my comment earlier. I've just never met a
man who is so conclusive about how someone manages their life
and their business."

"Apology accepted," Walter said. "You have now seen how
I deal with problems. Few have ever seen this side of me, aside
from maybe Leonard Schultz…. and now you."

Another unique side of Walter, Duncan thought. *So this is what
success feels like.*

❖   ❖   ❖

They sat there a little longer, had a snack and then left to
check into their rooms. The desk manager thought it odd that
they didn't have any luggage, but let it go for the moment.

Walter noticed the desk Manager looking for his luggage and
quickly said, "Our luggage was lost by the airline. Who knows
where it went," he added, trying to sound cavalier.

That seemed to satisfy the desk Manager, who tried a forced smile, but did not succeed. They walked through the lobby of the highly polished white marble floor, and past the oversized colorful pots, filled with expertly trimmed enormous queen palm trees. They walked into Henry & Poole's one of the exclusive men's clothing stores in the hotel.

"This is one of my favorite clothing stores," Walter said. "Get what you need for the next couple of days and a small suitcase and let's go up to our room."

Duncan felt like a kid in a candy store as he picked up items. *To think, I almost gave this all up,* he thought.

❖   ❖   ❖

Fred started doing some checking on Janus Parn. Other than the normal business dealings at the bank he worked at, everything seemed in order. However, just as he was about to finish his report, he found an article in the local paper from almost thirty years ago. It said that after the war Janus was institutionalized due to paranoia from being in a concentration camp.

He came home one night and supposedly killed his son in a fit of rage because he believed his son was in the Nazi Army as a young cadet. The police felt he had a relapse from the war and released him after six months to a sanitarium. His wife Mariana, was devastated, but felt that she had to stay with Janus.

When he was released from the hospital, six months later, he went back to work, as if nothing had happened. The neighbors where they lived were now aware of what he did, because of the newspapers. As a result, Janus and his family moved several times to a new town and finally settled in Tallin, Estonia. He went to work at Estonian Savings and Loan Union as a loan officer. His wife, knowing what he went through during the war, supported him, but was concerned he would one day have a relapse.

Chapter

40

It was now midnight, the perfect time to break into the museum. Paul was euphoric with excitement because he was in his element again. He was delighted that he could once more put his skills to good use. He still had bad memories of the last time he was at the museum, because he was caught, and went to prison. He was not going to make that same mistake again.

On this particular night, there was a moon out, which made it easier to hide in the shadows. Paul cautiously walked towards the delivery door at the back of the museum, and put on his black ski mask. He used his skills to pick the lock. *So far so good,* he thought. He walked in, hugging the wall in case there were any surveillance cameras. He worked his way to the stairwell always looking for cameras that could give away his presence. He wore his favorite black jeans, turtleneck sweater, and his black crepe soled shoes. Only his piercing eyes were visible though his ski mask. The custom-made thin leather gloves he wore did not leave any fingerprints.

He cautiously worked his way down to the fourth floor constantly looking around the room for any security devices. It had been over ten years ago and he was being cautious to make sure no other types of security devices had been installed since then. He pulled out a small can of hair spray and sprayed the area in front of him to see if he could detect any laser light security and found none. He went to a door with the name "MUSEUM STORAGE", stenciled on the door in big bold letters.

He again picked the lock and opened the door quietly. Inside, he saw numerous boxes and large crates piled high against two walls. He went in the door and locked it behind him. Now it was pitch dark, until he turned on his pen size flashlight. The crates and boxes were dusty and didn't seem to have been touched in many years. *I wonder why they still keep this stuff,* he thought. *The dust must be inches think in some places.*

❖   ❖   ❖

What Paul didn't realize was that when he picked the lock of the storage room, a silent alarm went off in the guard station in the main lobby of the museum.

"Hey Claud," said the guard in a guttural voice. "It shows on our monitor that the door to the storage area room has been opened. Go down and check it out." *Nobody has a name like Claud* he thought and chuckled to himself.

"Okay I'll go," said Claud. "But next time, it's your turn to check things out."

"Yeah, yeah, yeah," said the guard as he continued watching a soccer game on a small television screen.

Claud, armed with only a flashlight, started the long walk to the stairwell that would take him downstairs to the storage vault. He finally got down to the fourth floor, huffing and puffing all the way, since the elevators were turned off after hours. He stopped, and leaned against the wall to catch his breath. He saw it was dark except for the occasional lighted red EXIT signs. He walked over to the storage room door and tried to open it – but it wouldn't open.

He unlocked the door using his own key, went in, and shouted out, "If there is anybody down here....show yourself." *This is the only door to get in or get out,* he thought. *And, there are no windows to check.*

Paul was lying flat on the highest stack of the largest crate he could find. *I hope he doesn't check every nook and cranny,* Paul thought.

The guard said softly, "Probably just a short circuit." The guard turned around, switched off the lights and locked the door.

❖ ❖ ❖

"I wonder how Paul is doing?" asked Walter. "I hope I didn't send him off on a wild goose chase."

"I'm sure he'll be okay," Duncan said, trying to reassure Walter. "If he's as good as you say he is he'll either come back with the scrolls....or possibly they weren't there."

"While that may be true," Walter said. "It doesn't give me any comfort if he doesn't succeed."

❖   ❖   ❖

It was now pitch dark again, and Paul couldn't see a foot in front of him. He turned on his pocket flashlight and continued the search. After searching for some time, he finally found four large crates thick with dust, labeled *Dr. Benjamin Fazihd*. He found a crowbar, went to the first crate, and only found it full of books, so he quietly put the lid back on. The next box he opened, forced him to take almost everything out to examine it properly, but still he found no parchment scrolls or anything that resembled them.

He went to the third crate and only found some ancient artifacts that didn't look authentic to him. *I guess even the curator has counterfeit artifacts,* he thought, so he put the lid back on and went to the fourth crate. In it, he found a large box, ornately inlaid with ivory, which had an unusual lock. *This should be easy to pick,* he thought. However, it was more difficult than he thought. Finally, he just broke the lock and found some papyrus scrolls inside. *I found something,* he thought. *The only problem is that I don't know if these are the ones.*

He put that aside and found two long cylindrical tubes with identical types of locks. As before, he also couldn't pick their locks. *I guess I'll just take them all,* he thought. He put the lid back on the crate. *Now to get out of here,* Paul said to himself. He now knew that the door was connected to a security system. He knew he had to open the door quickly, lock it, and jog up the four flights of stairs, while carrying three containers. *I can do this,* he thought. He opened the door, locked it behind him and started his hasty ascent up the stairs, taking two steps at a time.

He got to the first floor landing, looked around, and from across the enormous lobby he saw the same security guard who yelled out, "Hey you. Stop!"

The security guard's yell reverberated throughout the main hallway like an echo chamber. Paul waited until he was close enough, pulled out his Taser gun, and gave the guard a fifty-thousand volt shock and dropped the gun on the floor. The guard fell to the floor, still twisting on the floor as he left by the side door.

Chapter

41

"Walter," said Duncan looking at him. "I was just thinking. How much do you really trust Paul to bring you the scrolls if he finds them? After all they could be worth millions to any number of museums or private collectors."

Walter turned to him, put down his cup of tea, "I actually only trust him a little bit. I've also created a contingency plan in the event he decides to keep them for himself. But let's see what happens."

❖   ❖   ❖

That evening Duncan learned a little more about how Walter thought and acted in crucial situations. *However, what kind of contingency plan could he have made,* he wondered. *I was with him the whole time.*

❖   ❖   ❖

It was now after midnight and the streets were empty. Paul walked casually down the street, carrying the three containers he took from the museum. He spotted an old model Audi automobile that brought back memories of his younger days when he lived on the Riviera. He broke the driver's side window, hot-wired the car and took off for the Kensington Plaza Hotel. He parked a half a block away and walked the rest of the way to the hotel unnoticed. He went in the front door and directly towards the elevator. He got off on the ninth floor and went to Walter's room. However, as he was about to knock, a tall beautiful blond, walked up to him, and pretended to like him. As soon as she got within reach, she pulled a gun on him.

"Go ahead, knock on the door," she said with a sly grin. "And no hero moves."

"Normally, I start out my dates with dinner and a movie," Paul said trying to figure out who she was. "But I must admit I like the new foreplay proposition much better."

"Maybe later," she said smiling. "If you're still alive." She pushed her gun into his ribs.

Paul knocked on the door and after some slow shuffling of feet, the door opened and an older man with a grey beard and bald on top, wearing pajamas, was staring at them.

He stood there and asked, "Yes…can I help you?"

"I'm sorry to have bothered you," she said with a fake smile. "We must be on the wrong floor," and she started walking Paul down the hallway.

"Are you trying to make a fool out of me?" she quietly said.

At that specific moment a man wearing tennis shoes, crept up behind her and gave a quick pinch to her neck, and she went limp to the floor.

"Ah....thank you," Paul said, amused. "But, who are you?"

"My name is James. Walter thought you might need a little help. Let's go up to the next floor, to Walter's *real* room."

Bewildered, Paul followed James, who was carrying the female gunman over his shoulder like a bag of potatoes, up the back stairwell. They knocked on Walter's door and Duncan immediately rushed to open it.

"Hi Duncan. Hi Walter," said James. "You were right, Paul was being followed. Here she is," and he tossed her on the bed.

Walter looked at Duncan, smiled and said with a wink, "Contingency."

"Thanks James," Walter said. "Go through her pockets and see if you can find a French passport or any other paperwork?"

"I did find a French passport," James said. "Her name is Sophia Mediate. But how did you know it was French?"

"Just a lucky guess," Walter said as he looked at Duncan. "Is there a cell phone in her pocket?"

"Yes there is," James said. "Another lucky guess?"

"Let me see the gun she had," Duncan asked.

James showed him.

"Looks the same as what the other French girls were carrying," Duncan said.

"What other French girls?" James asked, now even more curious.

"There seems to be an endless supply of French women," Walter said, "who are trying to kill me."

Walter quickly scrolled down on her phone, until he saw that familiar phone number he'd called before.

He pressed the callback button and said, "Hello?"

"Hello, who is this?" Apollo asked.

"It's me again," Walter said, happily. "It looks like this is number nine, I think. Again either you're not training them properly, or they are not trainable. In either case, you still ought to consider a different line of work. By the way, I just love the type of guns you give your girls. Very unique."

"I'll get you if it's the last thing I do!" Apollo screamed loudly, and threw the cell phone against the wall, where it shattered into pieces. "I don't understand how he can last this long!" shrieking at the top of her lungs.

❖ ❖ ❖

"What do you want to do with her?" asked James.

"Tie her up to that chair with arms," Walter said. "Make sure she has a gag on her and we'll let the maid find her in the morning. Take her pants and shoes off and we'll throw them down the laundry chute when we leave."

Paul sat on the edge of the bed, bewildered, watching what was unfolding in front of him, still clutching the three containers tightly.

Walter, turning to Paul, said calmly, "Well, what did you find in the museum?"

"I found these three containers, but I couldn't unlock them," Paul said. "I managed to break the lock on this one chest, but I wasn't sure which of them were authentic, so I brought them all."

"Great!" Walter said excitedly. "Since you still found Dr. Benjamin Fazihd crates, I have to assume that these are the scrolls everyone has been looking for. We'll just give all of them to the museum and let them sort it figure out if it's authentic. I have a contact in the Egyptian Government who will gladly take a look and figure out if any of these are real."

"How do you know if they'll find the pyramid and not steal what's in it?" asked Duncan.

"I don't. But I also don't think they will. After all it *does* belong to them," Walter said. "However, I *am* worried about this General Sean Flannigan getting his hands on the contents and keeping them for himself. Next stop is Cairo, Duncan. James, you can come along also if you like."

"What would you like me to do for now?" Paul asked.

"For the time being – nothing," Walter said. "Do you have an easy way back to Frankfurt?"

"Yes I do," Paul said.

"Let's take a cat-nap, for those of you who need it. We'll leave in the morning," Walter said.

❖　❖　❖

The next morning, Walter was listening to the news channel on TV and heard

"The Sir William Sheffield Museum reported a break-in and potential robbery. However, the quick thinking of the security

team thwarted the individual. After an exhaustive check by the Museum Director, nothing appeared to be missing."

Walter smiled to himself and thought, *perfect.*

Chapter

42

They left the hotel in the early hours, with Sophia still tied to the chair. They dropped off Paul at the London Paddington Train Station.

"Thanks for your help, Paul," Walter said, "And stay safe."

"I will and thanks for inviting me to your party," Paul said, as he watched them drive off.

Paul walked up the steps to the ticket window to take the next train home.

❖   ❖   ❖

That morning they flew off for Cairo.

"James, we haven't talked in a while," Walter said as he sat back in his favorite seat in the cabin of the ship. "How are you doing and what's been happening in Rome, now that you are the main person for Steve in Europe?"

"We've built up the business, and I now have four other people working there," James said. "Two men and two women. I recruited the two men from the SAS. Top-notch individuals. The two women I recruited were from the United States. One was from the Secret Service and the other individual was at the CIA. They happened to be here on vacation together and we struck up a conversation. The next thing I know, they're telling me that life in the States is too mundane for them. I explained what we do and asked if they would like to live in Europe, and they said great. Steve and I worked out all the details and a month later, they landed in Rome."

"That's a great story, James," Walter said pleased that Steve's organization was growing. "And how about yourself? When are you going to settle down? I know you have a girlfriend in Florence, and you see her when you go to Italy and the King James Casino and Resort. I'm not judging, mind you, and I think that's all wonderful."

"Well, I don't know if I'm the *settling down* type of person," James said, wondering how he knew that. "I've been involved in quite a few military missions and one of the things that keeps me going and wanting more – is the adrenalin rush with every accomplished mission. Right now, I'm still experiencing some of the rush. Nevertheless, I am also aware that as soon as the *rush* is gone, I may start making mistakes, and that's when I'll take a step back."

"That's very good and sound logic," Walter said. "I've always felt that you're only as good as your next replacement. By that I mean, you may want to consider looking for someone to replace you, and you can then work on the bigger picture and have your company grow. Just an observation, and if I can help you in any way, please just let me know. Remember what I said a long time ago, that you as well as Rick, Liz, Steve, Ernie and Fred, are all my children. As such, I want to help you achieve that dream. As you know, I'm now financially able to do the things that I could not have done forty years ago. I've known you for quite some time and you have been very loyal and instrumental in helping me achieve my goals."

"Thank you, Walter," James said, feeling a little chocked up, since his parents were both killed while in the military. "I'll keep that in mind."

"You do that," Walter said. "The offer is always open."

"What about you, Walter?" James asked. "When are you going to settle down and retire? I know you've accomplished a lot in your lifetime. When are you going to sit back and enjoy yourself?"

"My boy," Walter said. "What and how we do it, is what keeps me young. It's not the money so much. There is a certain thrill, when you can make something happen that affects hundreds, if not thousands of people. Being able to multi-task effectively is the key. As an example. We purchased a llama and alpaca ranch in New Mexico. This led to another llama and alpaca ranch in Bolivia. As part of the Bolivia ranch, there was a unique substance created by the Quechua Indians tribe in Bolivia that uses the shell of the Brazil nuts. They crushed the shell, added some other ingredients, and created a liquid they add when they washed and dyed the sheared wool of the llama and alpaca, which makes it almost as soft as cashmere."

"That's fantastic," James said.

"Then we made a deal with the Bolivian Government," Walter continued, "To sell them the actual Brazil nuts. Some of which they sell to a company who processes them into an oil-like substance. They sold it to several of the biggest watchmakers in Switzerland as a lubricant for movements. The rest of the nuts are sold for eating. Then we purchased a company in Tel Aviv that we converted from making cloth for the fashion industry into producing some very fine Persian-style rugs. This was all accomplished over about two months."

"Wow, that is terrific!" exclaimed James.

"Take your shoes off and stand up," Walter said pointing to the carpet on the floor.

James did as he was asked.

"You are now standing on one my new specially made rugs," Walter said. "What do you think? How does it feel?"

"My goodness, this feels just fabulous," James said, squeezing the luxurious material between his toes. Even through his socks, he could feel the softness.

Duncan listening to the conversation and was in awe at what he just heard. *Another part of Walter's life, I didn't know about,* he said to himself.

"Now you have a better understanding why I do what I do," Walter said. "In the end, it's fun in a way."

Chapter

43

Duncan landed at the Cairo International Airport around noon, and found the weather scorching.

"I'm not sure I can ever get used to this weather," Duncan said, taking off his jacket.

"There will be other things in life that may bother you," Walter said. "Good thing we're only here for a few hours."

They drove over to the office the Minister of Cultural Affairs and all Archeological findings.

They walked up the steps to a non-descript building that had a small brass sign next to the door Minister of Cultural Affairs. They were met by two heavily armed soldiers wearing crisp uniforms with a Task Forces shoulder patch from Unit 777.

Duncan noticed they both had an Israeli 7.62 Galil model machine gun strapped across their chests. *Lots of firepower,* he thought.

"We are here to see Akar Sekhmet, the Minister of Cultural Affairs," Walter said. "He's expecting us."

They were escorted inside. Soldiers were standing at attention on each side of the door. The guard opened the door with Akar Sekhmet's nameplate in polished brass.

"It is a pleasure to meet you, Mr. Donleavy," said the Minister." I want to thank you for recovering these precious papyrus scrolls."

"You're very welcome, Minister," Walter said as they sat down in his expansive office.

"You must understand," said the Minister, "we have known about the existence of the scrolls and what they mean. We just didn't know where they were located. What you are *not* aware of is that King Sekhemkhet is a direct descendant of our current King Rashaad Ahmed. It could become embarrassing if all this were to come out just as we are having a new election."

After much discussion, Walter was dismayed at what he had found out. They chatted a little longer and Walter was discouraged that the Minister didn't even open the box and look inside.

"Again, I want to thank you on behalf of the Egyptian Government," said the Minister.

"There have been lives lost over those papyrus scrolls," Walter said. "So please keep them safe."

❖ ❖ ❖

As the Minister watched Walter leave, he breathed a sigh of relief, and closed his doors. He took the scrolls out of the boxes and put them in large brass cauldron. He lit a match, and after saying something aloud in Egyptian Arabic, he slowly watched them burn until there were only ashes left.

The King will thank me for this, he thought.

❖   ❖   ❖

"Well how did it go with the Minister?" asked Duncan.

"He took the containers and oddly enough, he had a key that fit into the lock of the containers," Walter said. "However, he didn't even look at them. I assumed he would be excited, especially since I told him that I do not want any compensation or recognition as the finder for them. He did however tell me that they have *also* been looking for the lost pyramid. But not to find it, but to make sure it is *not* found."

"Why would that be?" Duncan asked perplexed after all the time and money Walter invested in this project.

"It has something to do with politics," Walter said dryly. "Evidently the king at *that* time when the pyramid was built was not a very good king. The current King's lineage goes all the way back to the old king of Egypt and they would rather not dredge up the whole story."

"But why? This is history, and I would have thought they would relish the idea," said James.

"You would think so," Walter said. "But in those days, that particular king was having an affair with his very own sister. Nobody seems to know if he ever had children. They have never found any records to prove or disprove this. In any event, the case is closed and it's now their problem. I'm happy that I was able to recover the scrolls in remembrance of my good friend General Metcaff. My only problem now is that General Flannigan may keep pursuing this."

"How will you stop him?" asked Duncan enthusiastically.

"Don't know yet," Walter said. "Need to think about this some more."

Duncan watched Walter go into a trance-like state and was afraid to interrupt his thoughts.

"On the other hand, I was still happy that we were able to meet with the Minister of Cultural Affairs," Walter said. "He was most appreciative for the scrolls and told us to come back anytime."

Chapter

44

A week later General Flannigan received a report that indicated that the papyrus scrolls had been found and turned over to the Egyptian Government.

"How did they get them!" the General shouted. "I've been searching for those scrolls for years!"

"But general, they now have the scrolls and we can go back to our jobs," said his Captain.

"It's not over until I say it's over!" the general said loudly, chewing on his cigar. "I want you to send a message over there to our contact, and find out how they got them. I don't recall any new archeological digs going on in Egypt. And I want to know yesterday!"

❖ ❖ ❖

General Sean Flannigan was a two star general. He had been in many campaigns, primarily administrative in Northern Africa. He graduated from West Point in the middle of his class. However, he was also very street-smart, compared to his fellow classmates in school. Upon graduation, He was initially assigned to an Artillery Division at Fort Bragg as a 2nd Lieutenant. He came from a privileged family and consequently his father was always pulling strings to get him special assignments to keep him out of harm's way. That was how he got the assignment in Northern Africa. He also convinced his close friend, Howard Metcaff, who graduated with him from West Point, to come with him.

The assignment was simple, with no special responsibilities, which gave them both plenty of free time to party and have a good time. However, after several months, they were getting bored. They decided to be daring and go into the bars that were considered off-limits to all military personnel. That night, dressed in civilian clothes, they decided to go into the Ali-Baba bar. They were drinking and having a good time when one of the girls, who was plying them with drinks was taunting General Flannigan

"Have you ever heard about the secret pyramid of Cairo?" she asked.

"No, tell me about it," Sean said, laughing, and feeling the alcohol take effect.

"Well, it's never been proven," she said, "But there are an-cient scrolls that show the exact location of this special pyramid. Nobody has seen it for over fifty years. I'm told by my father and his uncle, that it is much smaller than most of the other pyramids and contains priceless jewels."

"Go on, tell us more," Sean said, now excited, sloppily spilling wine on his clothes.

"The scrolls were supposedly stolen by the Nazis when they came through Cairo," she said. "After that, nobody heard what happened to them."

When she finished her story, he slid her off his lap and onto the floor as he stood up, and said to Howard, "We have a new task at hand, Howard. We're going to find those scrolls and that pyramid."

"Do you actually believe that bunk?" Howard asked, laughing and feeling no pain.

"Have you got something better to do?" Sean asked, grabbing the women who had been sitting on his lap before, and a bottle of wine. "See you in the morning."

Chapter

45

The next morning Sean went to Howard's room to wake him up.

"Rise and shine, buddy," said Sean jubilantly, because he had a new quest. "We're going treasure hunting."

"Are you really sure about this?" asked Howard. "After all, we still have work to do here on base."

"I'm very sure," said Sean excitedly. "The girl I was talking to last night took me over to meet her father and he told me a little more about this jewel encrusted gold crown. It definitely sounds real to me. Come on, let's go."

"All right, just let me get dressed," said Howard grudgingly. "I'll meet you downstairs in the coffee shop."

"Okay, see you then," Sean said, and took off.

❖   ❖   ❖

All Howard could think of lately was that he was potentially jeopardizing his whole military career. He had other ambitions. Moreover, being in North Africa was not his idea of a full military career. It was fun for a while, but at some point, it became boring. He finally got dressed and went downstairs to meet with Sean.

❖ ❖ ❖

"Okay, I'm here," said Howard. "Where do we go now?"

"You need to sound more enthusiastic," Sean said aloud.

"Yeah, you're right," Howard said. "Why don't we go see that girl's father again and see if he knows more about this special pyramid? I'd also like to meet his uncle, who has been around a little longer and see what he has to say."

"That's the spirit," Sean said beaming with excitement. "I actually already invited the two of them and the girl to this hotel's restaurant for a lunch. The girl said she would bring them. I may have to pay them something to get the information, but it might be worth it. What do you think?"

"I think that sounds good," Howard said, trying to sound enthusiastic. "But right now I need some coffee."

Shortly thereafter, the girl Sean met the night before brought her father and his uncle. They were wearing tattered clothes and barefoot. They looked as though they hadn't eaten in days.

Sean got up and said, "Hello there. It is so go to meet you again. Please sit down," as he gestured to them where to sit.

"Howard, this is Farouk and Akbar. These are the men I mentioned to you last night," Sean said.

"I'm pleased to meet you," Howard said dryly.

"They would like to eat first, if you don't mind," the girl asked.

While they all waited for the food to arrive, Sean looked over and saw someone sitting on the bar stool, occasionally looking in his direction. He knew he'd seen him somewhere before, but couldn't place him. He got up and casually walked over to him.

"I've seen you several times before," Sean said. "Are you following me?"

"Not at all. I frequent this place many times for lunch and dinner," he said.

"My name is Sean Flannigan. And your name?"

"I am the Akar Sekhmet, the Minister of Cultural Affairs and all Archeological findings for Egypt."

"That's why you looked so familiar," said Sean smiling. "You gave us a permit to dig in the desert a few years ago."

"Yes I did," said the Minister smiling. "I am very interested in what your three friends have to say about the pyramid they think they know something about."

"Well, you're welcome to join us," Sean said. "Come on over, let me introduce you."

As they walked over to the group, the girl's father and uncle saw the Minister, and with panic on their faces, excused themselves and tried to leave.

The girl saw the panicked look on their faces, when they saw the Minister and whispered to her father and uncle they should leave.

"I'm sorry, but we just remembered a previous engagement," she said, and pulled both of them out of the booth and almost ran out of the coffee shop.

"Now what was that all about?" Sean said as he watched them run off, leaving their lunch.

"I think you have been fooled by them," said the Minister meekly. "Those three have been spreading rumors about this pyramid I suspect, you are looking for."

"But she sounded so genuine," Sean said. "I can't believe we've been lied to."

"It seems that way," said the Minister. "I must go now."

"Well, it looks like it was as I thought," said Howard, sounding relieved. "Maybe now we can get ourselves re-assigned to state-side duty?"

"No. I'm not finished with this yet," Sean said. "You can go if you want to, but I'm staying a little longer."

❖ ❖ ❖

In 1985, Howard was re-assigned to the Pentagon, but after about six months, he was having some guilty feelings, about what Sean was trying to do in Cairo. He felt he had to tell someone. He found another fellow officer who had graduated at the same time from West Point, and is now an aide to the Chairman of the Ways and Means Committee. While they hadn't had much communication, he felt that he could count on him.

He met him over dinner at the Watergate Hotel, in Washington DC.

After a few drinks, Howard said, "In the beginning it was fun. But after a while he had this deep obsession in finding this mythical pyramid."

"I'm glad you came to me," said his friend. "I'll look into this personally. So Sean is still in Cairo?"

"As far as I know," Howard said.

They finished dinner and Howard now felt like a giant weight had been lifted from his shoulders.

❖　❖　❖

Six months went by, and one day Sean showed up at Howard's office at the Pentagon.

He burst into his office and said, "I can't believe you would divulge what we were doing over there in Cairo! I helped get you promoted and took care of you, when you were having problems at West Point. But don't worry this isn't over…not by a long shot. I'll get you for this." Then he stormed out of his office.

Unbeknownst to Howard, the person he had dinner with was also a very good friend to Sean. Now he was very worried, since he still had a lot of political influence with some highly ranked members of Congress.

Chapter

46

"It's so good to get back home to Monarch Ranch," Rick said, as they drove through the overhead archway that identified their ranch.

"Yes I agree," Liz said. "We've been flying a lot these past two years. I don't know how Walter does it."

"Always remember, that Walter is driven by an entirely different set of standards," said Rick.

"I got that same feeling," Frank said. "And I was only around him for two days. He is a very intense individual. But I guess that's what makes him so successful."

❖ ❖ ❖

As they were driving up the long driveway towards the main house, a pair of binoculars were trained on them.

"This time, we're going to take our time and watch when they are most vulnerable," said Roberta.

"Yes, that's right," said Lisa. "Apollo said if we don't succeed....not to come back."

"Well then, Lisa....I guess we shouldn't fail," said Roberta, matter-of-factly.

They both sat down among the rocks and trees and started to drink bottled water. The stillness was shattered when a bullet went through the bottle Lisa was drinking from.

"What the heck?" Lisa shouted, as she dropped flat on the ground, rolled down the small incline, and froze. "Roberta come down here!"

"Who could have known we are here?" asked Roberta, as she rolled down the hill.

"I don't know. But let's get out of here, now!" Lisa said.

They took everything with them, ran the quarter of a mile to their jeep, jumped in, and drove off.

❖   ❖   ❖

"There they go," Thomas said smiling.

He dialed Rick's phone. "Rick, you and Walter were right. I think they were doing more than just sightseeing. Looks like they're heading back to town."

"Thanks, Thomas," Rick said.

"No problem," Thomas said. "I saw a jeep in the hills that didn't look like it shouldn't have been there, so I put a GPS tracker under their rear bumper. I'll give them a few minutes and track them down, to see where they went from here. From what I can tell so far, they were both women."

"That's interesting in itself," Rick said. "Be very careful. This might be part of that same team from Billings. They may have followed us home. If you do happen to find them, you might want to search them. If you find that both have a French passport, a special .22 caliber pistol with a built in silencer, and a ticket back to Paris…then they are the same people or at least from the same *club*."

"Will do," Thomas said. "I'll call you with any updates."

"Thanks Thomas," Rick said, and hung up.

"What was that all about?" asked Liz.

"Oh, just some French sight-seers on our property," Rick said jokingly. "They may have followed us out here. On the other hand, they might be some other friends from their same *club*. I had Thomas to be on the lookout for anything unusual around the ranch – and he found them."

"They seem to be everywhere," Liz said, turning to Rick.

"Now where were we?" Rick said as he reached over and kissed her hard on the lips.

❖   ❖   ❖

Thomas Harrington worked for Steve Weisen, as part of the Weisen Security Team on the West Coast. He was also an ex-marine who had been in several successful military campaigns as a member of the Navy Seals. He met both Steve and Ernie on one of his many assignments in South America. He found out they were both born in the same town of Rossville, Mississippi.

"What a coincidence," Thomas said, joking.

"Yeah, now I know why I liked you so much," said Ernie in his make-believe drawl.

They ended up with different assignments, and after a while, they lost touch with each other. Thomas stayed in the service, promoted to the rank of Captain and considered staying until he retired. He became a company commander of E Company, 10th Engineers, 3rd Infantry Division. It was an ARCE (amphibious river crossing equipment) unit stationed in Kitzingen Germany. Things were going well, especially since it was a mechanized unit. They had more administrative field exercises, unlike the Infantry and Armored units that had military exercises constantly.

However, even in those days, politics were being played, and that's something Thomas did not do well. The Post Colonel found out, reading his file, which he'd been on several covert missions that were considered top secret. He wanted to know what they were, because he himself had never seen action. However, Thomas couldn't tell him about the missions, because they were classified and on a need-to-know basis. That riled up the Colonel, so every chance he got, he made life miserable for Thomas to be an effective company commander.

After a while, Thomas figured he had enough time in the service, so he contacted one of his friends, General Albert Lincoln. He was a three-star general, and his previous Company Commander, who sent him on those special missions. He asked him as a favor to process his papers for retirement from the service.

"Are you sure you want to do this?" asked the General wondering what was behind this.

"Yes sir, I think it's time," Thomas responded. "I'm afraid if I don't, I might do something I'll regret and that wouldn't look good. Making license plates in Leavenworth doesn't excite me."

"Okay, I'll take care of it," said the General. "But you know your Colonel is going to be upset about this."

"That's okay Sir," Thomas said, "I'll risk it."

The fact that his orders to retire from the service were generated out of the Pentagon, did not sit well with the Post Commander. However, he couldn't do anything about it.

When Thomas went to get his discharge papers, the Colonel, said arrogantly, "You don't like me very much, do you? I'll bet when I'm dead, you'll stand in line to piss on my grave."

"Sir, I told myself that when I left the service I would never stand in line again," Thomas said.

He saluted, took his new discharge papers and left the room. Within two weeks he was back home in the states. *I never realized how much I missed freedom,* he thought. He was able to reconnect with Ernie, who told him that Steve was creating a security company.

"Give him a call," Ernie said, "I'm sure he'd like to hear from you."

"I'll do that Ernie," Thomas said, "And thanks a lot."

Chapter

47

Monarch Ranch consists of about twenty thousand acres. It was originally named as the *Red River Ranch*. Walter purchased a company and this was one of the assets. He asked Rick if he would like to manage it for him. After he agreed, they renamed it the Monarch Ranch.

The main house had about twelve thousand square feet of living space. Eight bedrooms for guests; a movie/TV room that seated twelve; with satellite TV; a billiard room; ten-seat bar, with two card tables; and enormous elk antler chandeliers over the pool table. Another, even larger set of elk antler chandelier graced the foyer, and the dining room. It also had a twelve-foot-wide balcony on the second floor, which encircled the entire house, furnished with chairs and tables for all. This allowed all the guests to meet for cocktails. At the northwest corner of the balcony, there was a full bar that when not in use, rolled into a space in the outside wall.

There was separate housing for the ranch hands that, unlike the Old West, gave each one their own room and bathroom. They lived in spacious surroundings and had separate rooms for the twenty-five ranch hands needed when the time came for the cattle roundup and branding.

This was all converted from a guest cattle ranch for clients to spend weekends to relax, go hunting or fishing. Rick converted it to a full working cattle ranch to service the new restaurants Walter was planning to open soon. Initially Rick would only fly out on the weekends, but soon he came to like it and decided to move permanently to the ranch. They purchased more cattle and began the process of hiring more wranglers to manage the cattle.

While Rick was driving around the property one day, he found a large building on the north side of the property.

"This looks like a perfect place to have a meat processing plant," Rick said.

As he drove around further he also found an old spur line that went directly behind the old building.

It just gets better, he thought. *My guess this hasn't been used in quite some time. I don't even know if it is on my property.*

❖ ❖ ❖

After researching it, they decided to build a meat processing plant on the property adjacent to the spur line.

"This is going to be perfect when I buy those restaurants we talked about," Walter said.

"Walter, we just barely got through converting the ranch," Rick said. "Remember it was almost like a *dude* ranch for the wealthy and affluent clients the previous owner had."

"I know," Walter said. "But this was part of my long term plan all along. I've been reviewing some of the new restaurant chains."

Chapter

48

"How about a good long soak in the tub? I'll even turn on the bubble machine, with real bubbles," Rick said, laughing. "Remember, we have twelve jets massaging us the whole time. Plus, the refrigerator is only an arm's length away, stocked with wine and champagne."

"That sounds great!" squealed Liz. "What about Blueberry and Alexander? They're sitting in the doorway watching us."

"Let them get their own tub with jets," Rick said. "Besides this is our time."

Soon the soap bubbles spilled over the top slightly, but the kitties didn't move. They just stood in the doorway waiting for some of the larger bubbles to come their way. Soon they did, and they jumped up and started popping them. However, when the big bubbles stopped, they stood in the room and now *meowed*.

"I forgot the champagne," Rick said, as he stretched out over the tub and got his bottle of Dom Perignon with two glasses. "We *really* have to do this more often."

"I'm *always* ready," Liz said. "Maybe we should move the little fridge closer. After all…it does spoil the moment."

❖   ❖   ❖

Thomas followed the GPS tracking device back to town. He saw their jeep in front of the Wagon Wheel restaurant.

He walked in, sat at the bar, and looked around.

"Andy, have you ever seen those two ladies here before?" Thomas asked.

"They've been here almost every day for the last three days, just sitting in that corner booth," Andy said. "They're always whispering about something. This time they seemed a little irritated, as if they didn't get all their vitamins or something. Why do you ask?"

"Nothing special, just curious," Thomas said. "Give me a beer, please."

He sat at the bar pretending to drink a beer. After a few minutes, he grabbed his bottle of beer, left the bar, and swaggered over to their booth. He looked like one of the locals wearing cowboy boots, western shirt open to show his chest-hair, jeans, and his Stetson hat. He tipped his hat back on his head, which made him look like he just came from making a movie.

"Hi there, ladies," Tomas said in his country western drawl, as he sat down on the end of their booth. "You're new in town. Haven't seen you around here before."

"Yes, we are new here. We're trying to find a house we can rent for the summer," Lisa said, looking at a map of Fort Collins. "Do you know this area very well?"

"Yes I know it very well," Thomas said, and without skipping a beat, he said, "I also know that you two were in the hills, looking through your binoculars at my friends."

They were surprised, as they looked at each other.

"Don't even try to pull out your little *pea* shooter," Thomas said. "I've got a .44 magnum pointed at one of you. If you move a muscle, you'll wish you never came to Colorado. Now…why were you looking at my friends from the hills? I have a very bad feeling about you. However, relax, I know the Sheriff personally, as well as people in the CIA and the FBI. I'll bet they would love to talk to you."

"We don't know what you're talking about," Roberta said defiantly, in almost flawless English.

"Let's do this another way then," Thomas said as he placed his Stetson hat on the table. "I'll bet you have a French passport, a ticket back to Paris, a cell phone, and a .22 caliber gun with a built-in silencer in your pockets. Take em out….now!"

They looked at each other, wondering how he knew that. They slowly pulled the items Thomas said he thought they had.

"It's magic, how I knew this," Thomas said amused. "I'm going to give you one opportunity to leave this country. You can take your passport and your ticket….the gun stays here. How does that sound?"

They didn't know what to do, so they reluctantly agreed. "Why do you like them so much?" Lisa asked blazingly.

"Because they are very close friends of mine," Thomas said. "Plus he still owes me money from a card game from a week ago. Come on, let's go," as he slowly stood up and picked up their stuff and tossed it in his hat. They now saw his .44 magnum.

"Let's go out the front door," Thomas said. "My car is parked very close. By the way, if either of you are thinking of trying something, I have no problem blowing your head off. Please don't test me."

They walked outside towards Thomas' car. "Hold on there, while I open the trunk, Thomas said.

"You expect us to ride in the trunk of your car all the way to the airport?" Lisa said.

"Either it's that or we can continue walking to the Sheriffs' office and I'll sign an official document that you're both on the FBI watch list. By the time, they sort this out you'll still be in jail for at least six months."

"This trunk is filthy!" Roberta said, as she looked inside.

"Yeah I know. I've been meaning to get it cleaned out," Thomas said. "Now get in!"

They grudgingly got into the trunk of his car and he closed it.

Thomas drove them to the airport, but not before, he took some roads that had many potholes and windy turns through the hills. He finally came to an abrupt stop at the curb at the airport. He got out and opened the trunk.

"Okay ladies, end of the line," Thomas said as he opened the trunk.

They stared into the sunlight and had a few cut marks on their cheeks and hands.

As they were getting out, Roberta tried to kick out, hoping to catch Thomas off guard, but he easily deflected the kick and hit her in her calf.

"Ow!" she cried out.

"Let's not try that again," Thomas said calmly.

They both got out of the trunk and dusted themselves off.

"Just to make sure you get on that plane," Thomas said, "there is a guy waiting for you by the entrance doors. He will escort you to the ticket counter and then to the gate. He'll also call me if you've not made that flight. Goodbye, and have a safe flight."

They said, "You have not heard the last from us!"

"Actually... I hope for your sakes, I have," said Thomas. "What you're not aware of is that I have friends all over the world."

They shrugged their shoulders defiantly, started walking up the steps to the terminal, but looked back several times to see if Thomas was still watching them. As they entered the terminal doors, they were immediately met by a large fellow wearing farming overalls and a battered straw hat.

"Hello ladies," he said. "Right this way. And please don't be fooled by my clothes or my looks."

"Who are you?" Lisa asked.

"I'm your personal escort to see that you get on the plane," he said as he walked them to the ticket counter and then the gate. "Please have a nice flight.....and *don't* come back again."

He watched them walk through the long hallway, and boarded the airplane. The plane finally took off.

Chapter

49

"Well Walter, if there is nothing else, I'll be flying back home tomorrow," said Leonard dryly.

"I think you've done a fantastic job helping me reorganize my companies," Walter said, smiling. "I also talked to Liz, and she said that Jennifer Billingsly has accepted the position and will move out to Fort Collins by the end of the month."

"I'm glad to hear that," Leonard said dryly. "She was doing very well while I was at the office. Are you still going to try and buy any more companies?"

"Why do you ask?" Walter said quizzingly.

"Since you've divided up your company, you might want to downsize," Leonard said. "You have some very expensive real estate sitting only half used in a prime location."

"Yes, I have actually thought of that," Walter said.

"Thanks for the hospitality, Walter," Leonard said not looking at Walter. "Remember our deal. This was the last time we'd see each other on any of your business ventures."

"Yes, that was the deal," Walter said reluctantly.

They shook hands for the last time, and Walter walked Leonard to the front door, where Duncan was waiting to take him to his hotel. He watched Leonard walk down the steps and into the car, which he knew was for the last time. He felt sad as he said good-bye to not only his friend for over thirty-five years, but also as a business partner who helped Walter grow his empire. He watched them drive away and Leonard did not look back. Walter slowly walked back up the steps, through his foyer, and directly into his library. He closed the doors, because he wanted to sit in silence for a little while. As he sat there, staring out through his leaded glass window, he couldn't help but feel that Leonard was still harboring the pain of the loss of his son, Peter. *I guess I also feel that same pain,* he thought, *because Leonard will always think it was because of me, which drove his son to take his own life.*

"Mr. Donleavy," Hilda said knocking on his door. "Is there anything I can get you?"

"Maybe a cup of tea, Hilda," Walter said. "Also, are there any more pieces of the vanilla bundt cake with chopped walnuts left over?"

"Yes of course," Hilda said. "I'll be right back."

Walter sat there in his overstuffed chair staring out of the window until daylight had vanished. He thought about the day's activities. He went over them repeatedly in his mind and tried to convince himself that today was a good day. Somehow, though, he didn't feel that way. Something was bothering him, but he didn't know what it was.

❖　❖　❖

The next day Leonard was already seated, waiting for the plane to take off for his home in Switzerland, when he received a phone call.

"I think we should talk," said the voice on the phone.

Leonard hesitated for a moment, but exasperated, said, "I'm getting ready to take off for Switzerland. I could meet you at the Alpina-Gstaad Airport coffee shop on the ground floor."

"That's fine," said the caller. "See you later," and he hung up

Leonard sat in his first class seat watching from the window the baggage handlers load cargo. *I'll bet they're happier than I am,* he thought. *Then again, what would they do with a hundred million dollars?* He sat back in his seat, content that he wouldn't have to hear from or see Walter Donleavy ever again. He thought of happier times, when he first got married to his wife Cynthia. Then when his son was born, it was his second happiest moment. *I can't help it....I miss them so much,* he thought as he teared up. Suddenly he felt alone, because there was nobody to meet him at his home.

Just then, the flight attendant walked up and asked, "Can I get you anything, Mr. Schultz?"

"A glass of red wine, will do for now," he said as he looked up at her.

"Dinner will be served in about an hour after we take off," the flight attendant said.

"That will be fine," he said as he drank his glass of wine.

❖ ❖ ❖

Leonard landed at the Alpina-Gstaad Airport, close to Bern, Switzerland and after going through customs, went directly to the Alpina-Gstaad coffee shop. Soon, a second man sat down opposite him wearing an overcoat with the collar turned up and wearing a fur hat.

"Well, what is it?" Leonard asked irritated, because he had to wait.

"You asked me to sell all of your stock and other holdings and convert them to cash," he said. "If you sell all of your stock in Monarch Enterprises, you could create some alarm bells going off in the stock exchange. This could also get you investigated by the SEC."

"What do you recommend then?" Leonard asked.

"My suggestion is to sell off small blocks, so as not to attract any attention," he said.

"No! I want to sell my Monarch Enterprises stock all at once," Leonard said. "You're getting a sizable commission...so make it happen and do it on those dates I gave you," Then he got up and left.

Part of my job is to advise him, as his broker he thought.

❖ ❖ ❖

His broker kept wondering why the sudden urge to be completely liquid. He watched Leonard walk away towards a taxi stand and drove off. *I can't help but think this is a bad idea*, his broker thought. *However, it's his money.*

Chapter

50

Diana had some distressing news to share with Rick and Liz. She agonized for weeks on just how to tell them. She decided she would tell them the next time they both came down to have breakfast together. The day finally arrived, when Liz and Rick came downstairs and walked into the kitchen to have their breakfast. They noticed that she was nervous.

"Good morning Diana," Rick said happily. "How about you make us one of your favorite breakfast dishes that you know we like.'

"We'll be in the living room, so call us when you're ready," Liz said.

As they started to walk away, Diana said, "I need to talk to you both…please."

They turned to her, looking concerned, "What is it Diana, you look troubled….is everything all right?"

"Well yes, and no," Diana said. "Do you remember when I went on vacation to visit my children in Düsseldorf?"

"Yes we do. We thought it was great for you to do that," Rick said smiling. "Did something happen while you were over there?"

"Yes it did," Diana said, tearing up a little. "I went back to try and reconcile with my children. The more we talked, the more I knew I wanted to be with them. They have a terrific restaurant in Düsseldorf, called *The Alps Village*, which is doing quite well. They want to expand and open another place in the United States. They know I have a lot of experience in larger hotels and they have asked me if I would consider, at least for a short time, helping them start a new restaurant either in San Francisco or in Palm Desert, California. I'm going to try to talk them into the Palm Desert location. The air is much drier there."

"Why, that sounds wonderful," said Liz happily. "I hope you're going to go and help them out? You have an opportunity to be with your children and at the same time do what you love best."

"Yes, I agree with Liz," said Rick.

"Oh thank you for those kind words," Diana said, relieved finally. "I don't know how to thank you for all you've done for me."

To add some levity, Rick said, "But you're still going to make breakfast for us this morning aren't you?"

"Yes of course, I am," Diana said smiling, and feeling a heavy load lifted from her shoulders. "I will help you find and train someone to replace me. I have about two months before I have to leave for Palm Desert."

❖   ❖   ❖

Diana grew up in Croatia and Germany. She had been a secretary for a large ironworks firm and was doing quite well until World War II broke out. Everyone was scrambling and doing almost anything to feed the family. Like so many other young women in those days, she went to work at Messerschmitt Aircraft, as a factory worker, assembling the ME 262 airplanes used in World War II. A little later, she and her husband were caught hiding their cousin, a Jewish person in their house. The Nazis took all of them to Sachsenhausen Concentration Camp.

Helmut, her husband, because of his printing background, went to work with Adolf Berger, the master art counterfeiter. They could see that Diana had office skills and promptly sent her to work in the offices of the camp. She wasn't able to see her husband Helmut for several years. Luckily, they both survived, and found each other after the Russians came to liberate the camp, and everyone was set free.

Unfortunately, her husband passed away shortly after they were liberated, so Diana decided to leave and immigrate to the United States, not knowing if her children were still alive. She landed in New York and was fortunate enough to work in several four-star hotels in New York as a chef's apprentice. However, her specialty was European cuisine. Many years later, she found out from a cousin living in Germany, that her children had survived the war. She went back to Germany to try to see them and confirmed that they did survive, and were all grown up. They were living in Düsseldorf, Germany with some other relatives. She considered reconnecting, but felt that too much time had gone by and they probably wouldn't remember her anymore. Therefore, she came back to the United States and was doing what she did best, and still loving it.

❖ ❖ ❖

Diana had made a home for herself at Monarch Ranch, and immediately her life had more meaning. She was their housekeeper for almost five years. She had her own two room, bedroom and living room downstairs with her own private little kitchenette, and bathroom. She was reluctant to start a social life, because she still hadn't gotten over that her husband, Helmut, had passed away.

❖ ❖ ❖

"I'm really going to miss Diana," Rick said. "We've been through a lot just since I moved onto the ranch."

"I know what you mean," Liz chimed in.

"On the other hand, she will have a great opportunity to be with her kids," Rick said. "I wouldn't want her to pass up this opportunity."

❖   ❖   ❖

That night, Diana sat down in her bedroom and wrote a letter to her children living in Düsseldorf, Germany, telling them she would support them and help them start a new restaurant in Palm Desert, California.

Chapter

51

"Duncan, we need to find this Apollo and quickly," Walter said. "I also need to find out who and why someone has a contract out to kill me. In addition, Rick just informed me that two other French women were seen checking out the Monarch Ranch. All of these women seemed to be well informed – perhaps too well informed."

"This is the second major attempt on your life since I've met you," Duncan said trying to understand Walter's life so far. "Could it be jealousy of a competitor?"

"No, I'm afraid not," Walter said wryly. "I think it's closer to home." It reminded him of when he was on the run as the war ended. Even though the war had technically ended, there were still small groups of rogue military soldiers that thought the war should never have ended.

"Mr. Donleavy….Hello?" Duncan said.

"Yes what is it," Walter asked.

"You were zoned out there for a few minutes," Duncan said.

"Sorry about that," Walter said. "I was just recalling my time before I came to the United States. I was running and running, never knowing when or if I would eat or where I'd sleep that night."

"I had no idea about your past," Duncan said, surprised he was willing to share something about his previous life.

"Alana was very helpful yesterday," Walter said, trying to change the subject.

"Would she really have died, with what Aki did with those two pins?" asked Duncan.

"I told you earlier that was just a show," Walter said. "However, Aki is very capable of performing the actual task. And yes,.... then she would be dead. Aki knows exactly where to insert those pins, to give you that feeling of genuine pain. It is more psychological than anything else is. Why do you ask? Are you squeamish about death? After all, I know you have seen death."

"No, not at all," Duncan hurriedly said, and just let the statement drift.

"Let me call James and see if he has any information on Apollo Bonnaire," Walter said. "I'm also going to call Fred and see what he may have found out from the French Sûreté and his friends at INTERPOL."

"That's a good idea," Duncan said, excited. "I guess that means we'll be flying to Paris to find Apollo?"

"Yes we will," Walter said firmly. "For now let's drive over to my restaurant, The Alpinhoff and have lunch. This will give me a chance to see my new general manager, Milton de La Cross in action."

❖　❖　❖

They drove up to his restaurant and he parked in their customary private spot in front. As Walter walked in, he was greeted by Milton.

"Welcome Mr. Donleavy," said Milton with a warm greeting. "I am so happy to see you. Again, thank you for giving me this opportunity. You won't regret this."

"I'm sure I won't," Walter said, responding positively.

❖　❖　❖

"Milton, it looks like you are doing well here," Walter said.

"Thank you Mr. Donleavy," Milton said.

"I know it's early, but have you considered who could be your replacement?" Walter asked.

Milton looked at Walter, wondering what he was referring to and whom he meant.

"Please don't worry, Milton," Walter said smiling. "I was merely suggesting a back up to you, similar to when Jacques trained you as his protégé."

"Oh I understand," said Milton, breathing a sigh of relief. "I actually have someone in mind. Her name is Leticia Wadsworth."

"You can never tell when another opportunity will come up," Walter said. "Always remember something. If you don't have a backup, it makes it more difficult to promote you. Who knows, I may just buy another restaurant."

"That's true," Milton said. "I'll start working on that," and they left to get their lunch.

"You scared him a little, Mr. Donleavy," Duncan said.

"It wasn't meant to scare him," Walter said. "It was merely meant for him to think outside of the box. That's what always help me grow my business."

Just when I think I have him figured out, he amazes me all over again, Duncan thought.

Chapter

52

Apollinaris Bonnaire, or Apollo, as she was called by her inner circle, was a young impressionable girl of fifteen, running around on the streets of Paris. Her parents had long abandoned her, and she was reduced to begging for food on the streets. She was almost arrested in Paris, trying to pick the pocket of an older man. He was eating his lunch by the Fontaine de la Pyramide, close to the Louve. She wasn't very good as a thief and he caught her right away.

"Is there something I can help you with?" asked the individual calmly. "If you're looking for money, you need a much better approach."

"I don't want charity!" she said defiantly, "And I will get money, so I can eat."

He looked at her for a moment, with dirt smudges on her face and hands. He decided to help her.

"Come with me and I will teach you how to never get caught and have to do this again," he said.

"By the way, what is your name?" he asked.

"It's Apollinaris Bonnaire, but my friends call me Apollo," she said. "What's your name?"

"My name is Paul Mathews," he said.

❖ ❖ ❖

She never found out about his true profession as a thief extraordinaire and that he had made his fortune stealing from the rich and famous. Their relationship seemed to click almost immediately and they developed a mutual trust for one another. He homeschooled her and taught her etiquette, how to dress, be womanly and how to eat with all the right utensils and of course, how to pick pockets and never be caught.

After about three months, he said to her one day, "This is all I have to show you."

"I just love this dress you bought for me," she said as she danced around the room showing it off.

"Here is a thousand Francs to do with as you wish," Paul said. "I must leave Paris for a little while and travel to London on business."

"Why can't you take me with you?" Apollo asked frowning.

"There are some things I must do alone," Paul said. "You may stay in this apartment, since it is paid up for the next two months."

❖ ❖ ❖

Paul left the next day because he had also started to have feelings for her. *In my business, it was a luxury I cannot afford*, he thought. He left without saying goodbye, went to the train station, and was on his way to London and the Sir William Sheffield Museum. He didn't do well there, because he couldn't keep his head in the game. Because he was careless, and were caught, he went to prison. That's when he met Walter.

❖ ❖ ❖

Apollo now felt empowered and felt she could do anything. She decided if she wanted the good life, she had to marry into wealth and power. She started crashing parties that were hosted by the rich, and was successful in getting herself invited to most events. On one particular occasion, at a masked ball, an individual came over and introduced himself.

"Hello. May I know your name?" he asked.

"It is Apollinaris Bonnaire," she said. "I seemed to have lost my escort. I guess I'll go home."

"My name is Andre Marquise, and this is my birthday party. How is it that I have never seen you before?"

"I just recently moved here from Lyon," Apollo said. "I must leave now," taunting him.

"Don't be so quick to leave," he said so eloquently. "Stay for a while and dance some more with me."

They danced all night and they had a wonderful time together. You dance beautifully," Andre said.

"My you have a beautiful place," Apollo said. "I have often dreamed of being in a palace like this."

"Maybe one day you will live in a palace like this," Andre said.

❖   ❖   ❖

Six months later, they were married and that was the start of her ascension to power. She learned to manipulate him and took as much money as she could from him. After a year, she decided to divorce him and with a quick settlement, she walked out of court a rich woman. She liked that power and now her ego was unstoppable.

She met another man, several weeks later, who said to her, "You are very beautiful. How would you like to put that talent to better use and make yourself a lot of money?"

"Who do I have to kill?" she quipped.

"It's interesting you should use those words," he said. "There is a lot of money to be made in killing people. However, you have to be good at it and never…..never be caught. I can teach you the fine art of assassination."

At first, it sounded too dangerous, but after giving it, a second thought, *Why not.*

Over the next several months, he taught her how to defend herself and assassinate people so it appeared to be an accident.

"You've come a long way Apollo," he said. "You have worked hard for the last three months and I have shown you a small amount about what I know. There is another man that can teach you even more. He lives in Taiwan."

He had gotten used to eating rich and expensive foods. He was usually drunk in the evenings and fell sound asleep in his favorite chair by the fireplace. A month later, the man suddenly died, but not before, she emptied his bank account.

❖ ❖ ❖

Apollo started recruiting for her new enterprise. She wanted people that were hungry for a better way of life. There were no boundaries for them. She made sure they were all single, good looking, unattached and preferably had no family. She hired a lawyer who was more street wise than lawyer-wise. Between the two of them, they recruited around fifty young women that fit their profile. They had to be smart, but not too smart and between the ages of eighteen and twenty-five.

She hired an individual from Taiwan who was a retired champion martial artist. She taught all the young women the fine art of self-defense, and all the various killing techniques they could handle in the short time she had to train them. After only thirty days, five dropped out because it was too difficult for them. After sixty days, six more left, because they didn't have the stamina required. After three months, only thirty-five women were left. The ones that left were never seen again.

"Your training has been an exhausting ninety days," Apollo said. "However, you are all to be congratulated for finishing this course. Each of you is now considered part of *The Team*. As such, I expect you to be loyal not just to me, but also your teammates. Your teacher, who is a grand master, will stay on and observe for another thirty days to see how some of you complete your assignments."

"I would also like to add that I have taught you only a fraction of what I've learned over the years," the grand master said. "Our time together was well spent."

"As a graduation present," Apollo said. "When you go back to your room, you will find new clothes and the keys to a new car. Rest well tonight, because for the next three days we will show you how to shoot a specially made gun that I've had designed as part of your equipment when you are out on assignments."

Chapter

53

Walter was sitting in his library listening to the International news when the reporter said,"

"Bernhard Krueger, a banker from Baden-Baden, was found by two hikers in a forest, dead, and buried in a shallow grave outside the city of Baden-Württemberg. He was shot in the head, execution style. To add to the mystery, his wife and three children have not been seen for several weeks."

Startled, Walter sat up in his chair, because he knew that name. This stirred up memories of when he was interned at Sachsenhausen Concentration camp. *This is too much of a coincidence*, he thought. *Moreover, I don't believe in coincidences.* He went to his vault and pulled out the red leather booklet that Ernie took from Kirk Odorkian last year. *There must be something in this book,* he thought. *I'll call Janus again. I hope by now he's had time to settle down.*

Walter dialed his number and after several rings, a woman finally picked up the phone and said, "Hello?"

"Hello. My name is Alfred Berger. Is Janus available to speak with me?"

"No. He is not at home at the moment," Mariana said. "Can I have your number and have Janus call you when he gets home?"

"Well, I'm not at home at the moment," Walter said. "I'm on my way to a business meeting. I've done business with Janus in the past, and I thought I would get his advice on a matter I'm working on. When do you think he would be back home?"

"I'm not sure, Mariana said. "He is on his way to Baden-Württemberg to see a client."

"Thank you. I will get back to him in a few days then," Walter said, and hung up.

❖   ❖   ❖

Janus finally got on the train to take him to Baden - Württemberg to see Bernhard Krueger. He anxiously looked around because he still had this feeling that someone was following him, but nothing happened. He sat and tried to relax for the long train ride. When the train finally stopped at his destination, he got off and noticed the news headlines about the death of Bernhard Krueger. He couldn't believe it. He looked around in a panic in case anybody was watching him. *This can't be happening to me,* he thought. *I have to figure this out.* He walked over to a small outdoor café and ordered an expresso coffee. He sat there with a clear one hundred eighty degree view of anybody coming in his direction. The more he thought about it, the more he thought it must be Alfred. *All of this started when he called me last week. I have to find him and settle this finally.*

❖ ❖ ❖

Walter put the phone down slowly and again thought about the coincidence. He went back to his red book that he got from Ernie and looked up any name with a Bad-Wurzburg address. He found only one – Ulrich Pasternoff.

Walter called Fred and said, "Fred I need another favor."

"Sure, what is it Walter?" said Fred.

"Find out everything you can on an individual named Ulrich Pasternoff," Walter said. "He supposedly lives in Baden-Württemberg, Germany. I think he is somehow involved in this puzzle to have me killed."

"I'll get right on it," Fred said. "In the meantime, and I know I don't have to tell you this, be careful."

"Thanks Fred," Walter said, and hung up.

❖ ❖ ❖

Fred started his research. He pulled up the name Ulrich Pasternoff as the President of Brandenburg Electronics, a major electronics company in Europe. As he dug deeper, using all of his resources, he found out that he was also a Major in the Nazi Army in 1943. He disappeared and was assumed dead or was a deserter, but was never heard of again. *That's interesting,* he thought. *There doesn't seem to be much information on him prior to 1965. Then suddenly he buys into an electronics firm, and within ten years, he becomes the President.*

He called Walter and gave him the information he had found out about Ulrich Pasternoff.

"He sounds like a very bad man," Fred said. "I don't need to remind you to be careful dealing with him."

"I will and thanks Fred," Walter said and hung up.

Chapter

54

Apollo was pacing the floor of her luxurious top floor office, getting frustrated at not being able to finish this one particular job. The word was getting out to some of her other clients that she was slipping and had lost her touch. Her ideas were not innovative enough to keep up with the latest security measures.

"I guess I will have to personally take care of this!" she said aloud. She walked over to her computer and started doing some deeper research on Walter Donleavy. What she found out was surprising. There was nothing available on him before 1954. She also found nothing about Alfred Berger.

"How can that be possible?" Apollo said aloud.

I will figure out for myself what I need to do, she thought.

She walked next door and opened two, floor length mirrored doors that went directly into her bedroom, and to her closet. She started pulling out clothes for her trip. Watching all this was her pure white Persian cat named appropriately – *Killer.*

"I'm going on a little trip," Apollo said to her cat, who made a faint *meow*. "But don't worry, Aurelia will be here to take good care of you."

She continued pulling clothes out of her closet and laying them down on her oversized round bed. *A ball gown in case I have to attend a party,* she thought. *In addition, of course my traveling clothes, leather catsuit with my high-heeled booties, along with my brimmed blue hat with a single multi-colored pheasant feather in the hatband.*

"Is there anything I can help you with?" Aurelia asked solemnly.

Apollo turned to Aurelia with fire in her eyes and said, "Nothing else.....just feed my cat! While you're at it, give her a bath and a pedicure!"

"Yes Apollo," Aurelia said as she turned around and walked back into the living room. As she did, she carefully picked up – *Killer.*

Apollo continued going through her closet. Soon her oversized round bed was completely covered from party clothes, to pant suits. *I just can't decide,* she thought. *What's happening to me?*

"I think you need help," said Aurelia as she walked back into her bedroom. "Please let me help you."

"Alright Aurelia," she said. "I don't know why I'm so lost."

Aurelia walked up to her, slapped her in the face, and said, "Stop your whining. Pull yourself together! This is a luxury you cannot afford!"

"You should not have done that!" Apollo said, massaging her cheek. "I could kill you for that!"

"Yes you could," said Aurelia with authority. "But how would that look if you started killing off your own team, because of a temper tantrum."

Apollo stood there in shock that anybody dared to challenge her.

"You're right Aurelia," she said and pulled out her gun from her carrying bag and shot her in the head. "You're right....I need to stop carrying on," and threw her gun on the bed. "*You* are a luxury that I can't afford either anymore."

She called, "Taniya," one of the other people on her team and said to her, "You have just been promoted as my new assistant and security. Your first job is to get rid of Aurelia, and clean up this mess."

❖   ❖   ❖

A shocked Taniya walked in, holding her hand over her mouth, as she looked at Aurelia laying on her back on the floor. She had a bullet hole in her forehead with blood oozing out onto the white chenille rug.

"I'll take care of this right away," Taniya said, tearing up and distressed that she had to do this to her fellow sister.

❖   ❖   ❖

Apollo started trying on some of her other outfits. Some of which she hadn't worn in a long time. She spent the next several hours trying on various outfits, including jewelry that had been given to her from former clients. She finally decided on four out-fits and had Taniya neatly packed by them into a large suitcase.

"Thank you Taniya," Apollo said, overlooking the incident that happened earlier. "When I get back, we'll sit down and talk about your future. I have plans to open similar operations in other European countries."

"That would be wonderful," Taniya said,

❖   ❖   ❖

Apollo suddenly felt she had renewed energy for the ordeal to take care of her most difficult assignment. She started by putting on her black leather catsuit, with a special alligator skin embossing. As she slipped into it, she felt a new sensation, equal to just shooting Aurelia. She slipped in her hands and arms and pulled the zipper up completely to her neck. She looked at herself in the floor length mirror and smiled. *I'm going to buy another suit just like this but in red,* she thought. She finished dressing wearing her short three-inch heeled *booties.*

Just then, Taniya came back into her room and said, "You look terrific! What else can I do for you?"

"Get my small bag down," Apollo said. "I will need some of my special *toys* for this job. Then find out where all my girls are and bring them all home. Call our lawyer to help you find where our girls are. He needs to start earning his money!"

"I'll take care of it," said Taniya and left the room.

❖   ❖   ❖

244

Duncan drove Walter to the Providence Museum. As they were driving, Walter was thinking about General Flannigan. He had to come up with a way to stop him from searching for the papyrus scrolls. He even entertained the notion that he may have had a hand in killing Howard.

They were going to have lunch at one of Walter's favorite little out-of-the-way restaurants.

"This General Flannigan," Walter said. "If all that we've found out about him is true, then he's a disgrace to the uniform."

"I agree with you, Mr. Donleavy," Duncan said. "However he's a powerful individual. It would require someone with more *stars* on his shoulders to stop him."

"You may be right, Duncan, and I may know such a person who might be able to help," Walter said. "I'll give this some thought, since this is such a delicate matter. I have friends in the Government, and I wouldn't want to involve them. However, I will seek their advice."

Chapter

55

Walter received a call from Fred regarding Apollo Bonnaire.

"Walter. I think I found out where Apollo hangs her hat," Fred said. "She lives in a castle named *Chateau de Carlson* on the outskirts of Paris. She has been losing clients over the last few months. I'm guessing it's – because of you and her inability to kill you."

"Thanks Fred. Fax me the address and anything else you have on her," Walter said and he hung up.

Within minutes, he had the fax with the information on it.

"Duncan. I need you to get ready for a trip to Paris," Walter said. "We may also be going to Germany, based on what we do in Paris. I'm going to call Ernie also and see if he can come with us. I want to leave by tomorrow afternoon."

"I'll take care of it, Mr. Donleavy," Duncan said, excited that they were going to Paris.

Walter dialed the phone. "Ernie, this is Walter. I'm going to Paris tomorrow afternoon. Can you free up your schedule to take a trip with me?"

"A trip to Paris!" Ernie said. "I'm in. See you at the airport."

"One other thing, Ernie," Walter said. "If you have any *friends* in Paris, you might alert them that we're coming over, in case we may need some hardware."

"Got it," Ernie said and hung up.

❖   ❖   ❖

Chateau de Carlson sat on a hill in the eighteenth district, on the outskirts of Paris. It was built in 1735 and once belonged to the Duke of Kingston, who had it built for his wife, The Duchess of Mulberry. It was complete with a dining room that sit fifty guests in the great hall and had fifteen bedrooms. It also included a dungeon deep in the cellar of the castle. The first year they got along famously. However, after a year, he tired of her and he couldn't get a divorce, because they were both Catholic. Therefore, he did what any Duke in his place would do – he had her arrested as a witch, which was punishable by death.

After he grieved for two weeks, he found another lover. This time his reputation preceded him and one day after drinking heavily, he bragged, and took his new mistress down to show her the dungeon, and show her his play toys. As he was showing her some of the torture devices, she took that opportunity to kill him with a knife to the heart. *I hope you rot in hell,* she thought. She dismembered his body and hauled him off in the dead of night, and dumped his parts into the Seine River. As she threw the pieces into the river, the current slowly carried them away.

It seems that his previous wife, the Duchess of Mulberry was her sister. She quickly renovated the place, and bought herself a different place in Lyon, France. From there the chateau changed hands many times and ultimately fell into disrepair, until Apollo bought it.

❖   ❖   ❖

The next day the three of them took off for Paris from the T. F. Green Airport in Warwick.

"Walter this is only the second time I've ever flown in your plane," Ernie said looking around at the plush seats.

"Is that right?" Walter said amazed. "Let's see, I purchased this plane about eight years ago and Steve was my pilot at that time. I think you're right about that. This is actually my second plane. The first plane I got was part of the assets of a company I bought in 1974. I traded up and purchased this one in 1983."

❖   ❖   ❖

Duncan listened to some of the conversation, and gained a little more insight into Walter's life. *That Walter is a real wheeler and dealer,* he thought. *I wonder what he has in store for me…if anything.*

❖ ❖ ❖

"What are you thinking of doing once we get to Apollo's chateau?" Ernie asked.

"I'm not sure we're going to her place yet," Walter answered. "I brought with us two of the cellphones they were using. Assuming Apollo still has the same phone number, I'll call her, tell her we're in Paris, and have her come to *us*. I'll make one more attempt to reason with her. If that doesn't work its all-out war until either she or I are dead."

"Let's hope it doesn't come to that," Ernie said taken aback by the comment. "I've got another idea that might work a little better. I'll need to get a few things at the *store* and then scout where her chateau is actually located and how fortified it is."

"Okay, let's go with your idea," Walter said happy for another viewpoint. "Now… let's see how we can stir up a little hornet's nest."

Walter dialed a phone number and asked, "Hello? Is this Ulrich Pasternoff?"

"Yes it is. Who is this? And how did you get this phone number?" Ulrich asked.

"Are you also the Major that was in the Nazi Army and disappeared towards the end of the war?" Walter said, taunting him.

"Who are you and how did you get that information?" Ulrich screamed into the phone.

"Does the name Apollinaris Bonnaire, better known as Apollo mean anything to you?" Walter said in a serious voice. "If it does….my name is Walter Donleavy," and he hung up the phone.

"Walter, you are one bad guy," Ernie said laughing after Walter hung up the phone. "He has got to be nervous as hell."

❖　❖　❖

"Hellena!" shrieked Ulrich. "Find out where Apollo is right now!"

Hellena dialed Apollo's phone, and finally after several rings it was answered. "Hello, who is this?" asked Apollo.

"It's me Hellena. Ulrich wants to talk to you," and she handed the phone to him.

"Apollo, I just received a call from none-other than Walter Donleavy!" Ulrich said. "He seems to know a lot about me! How can that be?"

"How did he get your number?" she asked.

"I don't know. But the bigger question is when are you going to finally kill him?" Ulrich yelled.

"I am in the process of taking care of this personally!" Apollo said boldly. "I'm still curious though, how he was able to get your phone number?"

"I don't know, and I don't care," Ulrich said. "All I know is he asked me if the name Apollinaris Bonnaire is familiar to me, and hung up! I hope you or your friends haven't involved me in any way, because if you did… your next chateau will be six feet underground!" He hung up and then threw the phone across the room, breaking it into pieces.

❖ ❖ ❖

Ulrich stood up from his oversized executive chair and looked out of his fifteenth story window and started to light one of his special cigars. He knew it wasn't good for him and his wife forbade him to smoke them at home. He paced his posh office, admiring his many awards he'd won for his company. Suddenly, they meant nothing to him because he was so angry and afraid. He sat back down and called the person that originally gave him the contract. However, nobody answered the phone. Now he was very concerned. *This can't be happening to me,* he thought.

Chapter

56

General Flannigan received some alarming news.

"I was just informed by one of our confidants in the Ministry in Cairo," said the Captain, trying to ease into the subject, "that the papyrus scrolls have been turned over to the Egyptian Government by an individual who has asked to be anonymous."

"What? I want you to contact our person in Cairo," said the General. "And find out everything he can about who accepted them, and where they came from."

"Yes sir," said the Captain trying to sound enthused. "I'll get right on it."

❖   ❖   ❖

The Captain left his office and went directly to the men's restroom. He went in and checked all the stalls to make sure they were empty, and then he locked the main door from the inside.

"What the hell is wrong with that idiot?" the Captain screamed aloud as he was clutching the sink bowl. *Doesn't he know that we have real live military business to work on?* He thought to himself. *I have to find someone to help me stop this madness without getting court-martialed. The problem is.....whom do I trust?*

❖ ❖ ❖

Apollo left her place dragging one large bag in her hand and walked to her private elevator that would take her to her personal garage three floors down. The doors opened and she punched the *B* button to get to her garage. As the elevator slowly descended, she thought about what had just happened in her bedroom upstairs. She was deep in thought when she heard the bell letting her know she had arrived at her floor. As the doors opened, she was confronted by a man standing directly in front of her.

"How did you get in here?" Apollo shouted.

"It was easy," Ernie said casually. "If you know how to pick locks."

"Who are you, and what do you want?" she demanded screaming.

"Possibly you're worst nightmare," Ernie said. "And I want you. However I can be civil about this....can you?"

By this time, her eyes were getting wide with hatred. She had lost her temper and made a quick grab in her purse, ready to pull out a gun.

However, Ernie was quicker. With one fell swoop, he knocked her purse down to the ground and slapped her so hard she fell backwards against the elevator doors and slid down into a sitting position. At that time, Walter came out of the shadows and introduced himself.

"Hello Ms. Bonnaire, or should we call you Apollo? My name is Walter Donleavy, the person you have been trying to kill."

Apollo sat on the floor in a trance, massaging her check, which by now was turning a very interesting shade of red. As she massaged her jaw, she felt a trickle of blood running down from the corner of her mouth. She had fire in her eyes as she tried to stand up.

"Please stay seated," Ernie said.

"I did tell you very nicely…several times in fact," Walter said. "To get into a different line of work. Based on what is continually happening, you did not heed my warnings. I'm going to repeat myself…..*but for the last time*!

"I totally underestimated you," Apollo said eyes wide open, while still rubbing her cheek.

"That's not what I want to hear!" Walter shouted, coming closer to her and bending down. "Do you know an individual named Ulrich Pasternoff?" Walter asked. He watched her facial reaction to the comment. He immediately saw the slight flinch in her eyebrow….that he hit a nerve. "Here we are at an interesting crossroads," Walter said as he stood up and turned away from her. "I made him an offer to have *you* killed. I said I would pay him

ten million dollars and then I never want to see or hear from him again."

"What?" she shouted. "He wouldn't dare!"

"Maybe he felt he had no choice….and I had to agree," Walter said nonchalantly. "I'll tell you what. He hasn't confirmed my offer yet, so I will make you the same offer, and I don't want to hear or see from you again either. Think about it. However… just too really be fair, I also have an alternative proposition for you. You could go away with Paul Mathews, who I know you know and live happily ever after."

"How did you find out about Paul Mathews?" she said, defiantly.

"I know a lot about you and Paul!" Walter said casually. "It's Paul who doesn't know that I know about you and him. Come on! Make up your mind! This is a one-time offer. On the other hand, I can just shoot you right now and my problem is solved. It's a win-win for me."

"All right…all right. You've made your point," Apollo said. "However, I don't have any idea where he is anymore."

"Here is the address where he works. Goodbye," Walter said handing her a piece of paper. They slowly walked out of the garage, with Ernie and Duncan walking backwards, with guns drawn, to watch Apollo.

Apollo sat there in the semi-dark garage, feeling abandoned with her six cars and a motorcycle. She finally stood up to contemplate what her next move should be.

Now I do know what I'm going to do! She said to herself.

❖ ❖ ❖

"I think she got the point," Duncan said thinking she'd take the last offer.

"No…I'm afraid she didn't," Walter said cynically. "Plus I don't want her involved with Paul."

As soon as they were clear of the garage door, the entire garage blew up with fire and smoke spewing through the broken windows of the six garage doors.

"Whoa! Did you see that?" Duncan yelled out.

"I don't have to see it," Walter explained. "I had Ernie set the explosives, so that if she turned the ignition on to any of her cars, it would create a chain reaction to the other cars. Remember the word…contingency."

"But what about the rest of her team?" Duncan said excitedly.

"They all knew the risks being in that line of work," Walter turned and said to Duncan. "I doubt seriously if any of them will come after me, or any of my close friends."

Chapter

57

Taniya and some of the other team heard and felt the explosion and rushed down the stairs to the garage. By the time they got to the garage level, the entire area was in flames. Fire Department sirens with earsplitting sirens, along with the Police, were trying to help put out the fire.

"Where is Apollo?" Taniya shouted out, but no one answered.

After several hours, the Fire Department said it was clear to go back into the building.

"There was a body the Police discovered leaning against the elevator doors," the Fireman said. "They seemed to think it was a female."

"Oh my gosh," said Taniya, starting to cry.

"What are we going to do?" asked one of the team members.

"I'll tell you exactly what we're going to do!" Taniya said boldly. "That last client...the one she's had so much trouble with…this Ulrich Pasternoff. I'll bet anything that he's behind this. I also know where we can find him."

❖　❖　❖

"Mr. Pasternoff, this is Walter Donleavy."

"Why are you still calling me?" Ulrich demanded.

"I understand there was some type of friction within your friend…Apollo and her group. In fact, I understand she's…. dead."

"What are you talking about?" Ulrich yelled into the phone.

"I heard it on the International news, just minutes ago," Walter said, and hung up.

"Don't you think he'll just contact one of the other women in Apollo's group to finish the job?" Duncan asked.

"No I don't," Walter said. "He's got bigger problems. My guess is that he's been paid a substantial amount of money for this contract. So far, he's *not* fulfilled any part of it. I also think he may have paid Apollo's group something in advance. Plus he knows that I know about his past as a high ranking officer in the Nazi Army."

"That still leaves some of the other team members of Apollo's group," Ernie said. "What are the chances they'll go after this Ulrich character?"

"I'm counting on it," Walter said with a sly grin. "Let's go home…I'm tired and I don't think we need to go to Germany."

Ernie just listened to how Walter thought and was proud to be a member of his team.

Chapter

58

Several weeks later, Duncan drove Walter to the town of Mystic in Connecticut to have lunch at the *Lobster Tail*. Walter knew it was a long drive just to have clam chowder. However, he had a second reason for the drive. He'd heard it might be for sale. He'd always wanted to have a separate restaurant to serve just seafood, and this would complement his other two restaurants. As they sat down at the table and looked at the menu, Walter looked around, and thought, *this place has potential*.

"Have the lobster corn chowder," Walter said. "I'm told it's very good. Tell me what you think."

"This is marvelous," Duncan said with enthusiasm. "It's rich and creamy and has large chunks of lobster in it."

"Well, what do you think Duncan?" Walter asked. "Should I try and buy it or pass?"

"You're asking me?" Duncan responded.

"Yes, I am," said Walter. "I don't know if you want to keep performing as my security all your life. You've eaten food from all over the world and by now you must have developed, hopefully, some good taste buds."

❖   ❖   ❖

Duncan remembered his own childhood being raised in Southern California. His parents came over from Sweden in the early sixties. They weren't used to American food and consequently his mother made many of the traditional foods popular and native to Sweden.

As he got older, he would ask his mother, "Why can't we have a hamburger or fried chicken, like the other families have."

She would say to him, "Those are expensive foods and we don't have the money for those frivolous things."

When he was in his teens, one of his friends treated him to a hamburger, "My goodness, this is fantastic!" he said.

From then on, he was hooked. However, it also took its toll. When he was in the ninth grade in high school, he started to gain weight. Soon, the other kids were making fun of him, because of his weight gain. He started to exercise, changed his eating habits, and now started to build muscle. After six months, he was a changed person. He got even more involved in bodybuilding and even had aspirations of competing in some of the bodybuilding contests. When he graduated from high school, those same kids were no longer laughing at him, but instead admiring him.

"I owe it all to you," Duncan said. "You made me feel like crap for a long time. Now I only have one thing to say to you all, *eat your heart out.*"

Shortly thereafter, he joined the Marines, which changed his world a little more.

Chapter

59

"Hello Rick," Walter said casually. "Are you and Liz going to be available over the next few days at your ranch?"

"Yes, matter of fact we are," Rick said. "What's this all about?"

"I'll tell you when I see you," Walter said. "I would like Fred to be available also. In addition, I'm inviting Steve, and Ernie to be there as part of the meeting. Don't worry I'm not dying, so hopefully you can have Diana make something special for dinner that day. I assume you still have room to have us all stay a few nights?"

"Yes we can accommodate everyone," Rick said happily.

"Thanks. See you in two days," Walter said. "Oh, one other thing, and just as a precaution. You should *sweep* your whole house, your cars, and all your clothes you frequently wear for any *bugs* you may have."

"Okay I'll do that," Rick said, and hung up. "I wonder what that was all about," scratching his head?

"I guess we'll find out in a few days," Liz said.

❖   ❖   ❖

"Steve, I need to visit with you," said Walter. "Have you moved your operation to San Francisco yet?"

"No, not yet, but soon. Why do you ask?" asked Steve.

"I would like to have a special meeting with you, Rick, Liz and Ernie at the Monarch Ranch," Walter said. "I want to talk about some recent developments that all of you should be aware of. Can we meet there?"

"Yes we can, Walter," said Steve. "Is there something I should know about to prepare for this?"

"No, not really," Walter said. "However, just as a precaution, you should check your house and your cars for any *bugs* you may have." And he hung up.

Walter made a similar call to Ernie.

❖   ❖   ❖

Steve met with Dorothy to see how things were going.

"Hi there," Steve said as he kissed her. "How would you like to go on a little two to three day vacation and meet my other friends in Fort Collins, Colorado?"

"I guess we could do that," Dorothy said, trying to smile a little.

Steve could still feel the tension in her voice. He had to tell her about Dennis Pristinely, so she could stop worrying.

However, Jimmy was a different problem and he wasn't going to tell him.

"I feel I need to tell you what happened to Dennis Pristinely," Steve said.

"Why…what happened to him?" Dorothy asked, sounding alarmed.

"Don't worry…I didn't kill him," Steve said. "I just put the fear of God into him. I don't think he'll be coming around to bother Jimmy or you anymore."

"I told you I didn't want you to get involved with this," she said. "This is our problem."

"I know," Steve said. "Nevertheless, I've met people like Dennis all my life and they wouldn't have stopped until Jimmy or you were dead. In any event, it's over and you can now sing your heart out and feel good again. I hate to see you unhappy."

❖   ❖   ❖

Dorothy had started out as an executive secretary in a very prestigious law firm in Boston. She was hired even before she graduated from college. However, after working a year in that job, she felt she wanted to do something else. While still attending college, she had sung in the glee club and had found that she loved it, but never considered it a full-time career. One evening, while on a date, they went to a karaoke bar and she was talked into singing a song. She was an immediate hit. Her date at the time convinced her to give singing a chance. She thought about it some more and decided to do it.

She started singing in the local clubs and developed a small following in the area. Soon after, she started being paid for her performance. She was very attractive, with dark green eyes and bright red hair. Between her voice, which was the envy of many of the women who tried to imitate her, and her looks, she was hard to beat.

❖ ❖ ❖

Dorothy went to Jimmy's office to talk to him.

She walked in and stood in front of his desk and said, "You don't have to give this guy Dennis any more money."

"What...what do you mean...what happened?" Jimmy asked shocked.

"Never mind. I took care of it," Dorothy said. "That means that I want *you* to start managing this place like a real club or I'll sell my share of this place to Dennis. Do you understand me?" And she left his office.

Jimmy didn't know what to think and just sat there with his mouth wide open, wondering what she had done.

Chapter

60

Janus left the café after sitting there for a full hour, observing everything and everybody in the café area and the plaza. He'd had so many cups of expresso that he was feeling more paranoid than ever before he left on the next train for his home. *I can't spend the rest of my life in this café,* he thought. He got up from his seat, paid his bill and started walking to the ticket counter to buy his ticket for his long trip home.

He walked to the terminal and sat on the cold wooden bench, waiting for the train to arrive. He thought about happier times, before the war, when he and his wife were living in a small one-bedroom apartment. Finally, the train pulled into the station, clanking its bell to announce its arrival. He boarded the train and went to one of the cars that seemed vacant of other passengers. He sat in a seat next to the door, with a full view of anybody coming down the aisle.

He went back to his thoughts and then they turned dark. He still remembered the day he and his wife were torn from their home in the middle of the night. They couldn't take anything with them, as they were marched into one of the train's cattle-cars. After a long train ride in a very crowded compartment, they finally ended up at one of the concentration camps. At the time, they didn't know where they were, because they'd lost track of which direction they were going. He finally found out that they were taken to Sachsenhausen Concentration Camp.

He felt a tap on his shoulder and a soft voice asking, "Excuse me, but is this seat taken?"

He suddenly came out of his daydream, looked up, and said, "No, it is not. Please sit down."

"Thank you," she said as she sat opposite to him. "My name is Hellena," holding out her outstretched hand.

"My name is Janus," he said, shaking her hand. "Where are you traveling to?"

"I'm going back home to Paris," she said, beaming.

"That's nice," Janus said. He sat there for a few minutes and quickly realized that she was on the wrong train if she was going to Paris.

"Now just stay quiet," Hellena said calmly, as she sneakily produced a small gun pointed directly at his chest.

"What's that for?" he asked calmly.

Hellena didn't answer, but just kept staring at Janus.

The train started pulling out of the station, with a jerking motion. Their car was still empty of other passengers. He had to think of something, but nothing came to mind. He couldn't believe that this was how his life was going to end.

Hellena broke the silence and said, "I know you're probably thinking....why me? I don't have the answer to that question."

The train started to pick up speed and you could hear the clattering of the train wheels on the tracks.

"How did you find me?" Janus asked.

"I can't answer that either," Hellena said. "But evidently it had something to do with Mr. Bernhard Krueger."

"How long have you been following me?" he asked.

"Oh, about a day or so," she said. "You spent so much more time in that café, that I couldn't get close enough to you."

"I assume you're going to kill me?" Janus asked in a matter-of fact way. "I can give you ten thousand dollars right now from my briefcase and you can walk away."

"That wouldn't be very ethical," Hellena said bemused by the offer. "However, I'll take the money anyway, because you won't need it…anymore."

The train rang its bells loudly, telling its passengers that they were going through a tunnel in the mountains. It got dark, but just before the emergency lights came on, a shot was fired with a deafening roar. A few minutes later, they came out of the tunnel. Hellena was slumped forward and Janus was nowhere to be seen. He had taken that opportunity to move to a different car, which was more populated. He suddenly felt better around other people again. He listened to them talking, and having a good time. Some were even singing.

❖ ❖ ❖

Why hasn't Hellena called me yet? Ulrich thought. *I'll give her a little more time.*

Ten minutes went by and then twenty minutes, and still no call. He decided to call Hellena.

He dialed her number and after the third ring, the phone was answered.

"Hello? Who is this?" asked the Officer in a gruff voice.

Ulrich disconnected without saying a word. Now panic started to set in. First, it was Apollo, now it was Hellena. He got up and paced his office floor like a caged animal in a circus, with nowhere to go.

It must be Alfred Berger, or whatever he calls himself, he thought, frustrated because he couldn't contact anyone. He sat in his chair, and pulled a gun out of his drawer. He lay the gun on his desk, and started writing a letter to his wife. Suddenly the phone rang.

"Is this Mr. Ulrich Pasternoff?" Taniya asked.

"Yes it is," he said.

"My name is Taniya," she said. "I used to work for Apollo. Our final act will be to destroy you, for what you did to Apollo!"

"What are you talking about?" he screamed into the phone. "I paid her a lot of money and we have been partners for years!"

The phone went dead on the other end.

❖　❖　❖

Janus took the train and the trip was uneventful until he got to the next station. As he looked out of his window, he saw several police and an ambulance parked on the station platform. He sat there oblivious and tried to stay calm while they went through the train. They passed by him and didn't stop, so he felt he was safe.

He continued his journey and finally got off at his stop in Tallin. As he got off, he for some reason did not feel paranoid anymore and walked briskly to the trolley that would take him home. He got off the trolley, walked the two blocks to his home.

He walked in, saw his wife and that's when she said, "A person named Alfred Berger called for you. He didn't want to leave a number, but said he would call you back."

"Thank you dear," he said.

Now suddenly he didn't feel safe again. *I wonder what he wants now,* he thought. *I have to find him and find the underlying cause of why he called me.*

His wife looked on, a worried look on her face. It brought back memories of when he was sent to the sanitarium after his son was killed.

❖   ❖   ❖

"Let's go girls," Taniya said. "We have a long trip to Baden-Württemberg."

Chapter

61

"Mr. Chen, this is Ernie Slater."

"Mr. Slater, it is good to hear from you," Victor said.

"I'm in desperate need of some rest and relaxation," Ernie said. "Or as we call it in the Army R & R. Are my two favorite *friends* available when I fly over there tomorrow?"

"I will personally see to it that they are available," Victor said. "I will also send my car to pick you up when you arrive."

"Thank you so much," Ernie said. "I'll call you with my flight plans," and hung up.

❖ ❖ ❖

Victor Chen was the head of an organization called The Li Chan Group. Originally, the Xingang families were primarily located in the Nanchang Provence of China. The Chinese Civil War broke out, which lasted ten years. The surviving members of the Xingang family had smuggled gold bars and jewels out of China and into Sapporo, Japan. They stayed in relative hiding until the war was over. There was the father, mother, two daughters, and five sons, which made up the family. The father and mother died before they could go back to their homeland and restart their life. However, the seven surviving children created a powerhouse organization called – The Li Chan Group.

Once the war was over, the family tried to go back to their home. The war partially destroyed the family home, but the land was still there. However, because it was considered *spoils of war*, General Xingcho confiscated it. The Xingang family asked if they could buy it back, but he just laughed and refused. Within two days, they had a signed bill of sale from the General for the property and the General was never seen again.

The family developed a reputation in the region for helping other families with similar problems. Their fee for this *help* was nominal, because they wanted them as friends and allies. Soon they had developed strategic relationships with many of the more prosperous families.

❖   ❖   ❖

Their families all chipped in, had enough money to invest, and opened a casino nightclub called *The Washington*. They named it *The Washington,* because they wanted to attract U.S. visitors who had more money to spend. It served as a hotel and casino, and within five years, they opened two other hotels and casinos in Macau.

They grew into eight families – and all part of the Li Chan Group. The group kept a low profile and slowly started buying surrounding land and property for future projects.

❖   ❖   ❖

Walter met Victor Chen, when they were both competing for the same Hotel and Gambling Casino in Johannesburg, South Africa.

Walter asked Victor, "Could I interest you in building the most fantastic and luxurious Casino and Hotel Resort and mega-mall in all of Africa?"

Walter ultimately sold his interests in the hotel to Victor Chen. However, their relationship blossomed from that point on.

Chapter

6 2

That evening, Walter took one of the golf carts and drove over to see Aki Watanabe at his home on Walter's estate.

Walter knocked on his door and said, "Good evening Aki," and bowed to him.

"Good evening Mr. Donleavy," said Aki. "It is an honor that you have come to visit us. However, I sense you come with a heavy heart."

"Yes I do Aki," Walter said. "I need something very special, that I think only you can prepare for me."

"Whatever you like Mr. Donleavy," Aki said. "Please come in and sit down. Would you like some tea...we have your favorite?"

"That would be lovely," Walter said solemnly.

After the tea came, Aki's wife, Tomichi, excused herself and left the room. Walter explained in detail what he would like Aki to prepare for him.

Aki sat there for a moment and thought.

"I have not prepared anything like this for many years," Aki said. "However, I'll create this for you. I have to go into town for some of the items I need."

"Thank you Aki," Walter said. "I am in your debt for this."

"On the contrary, Mr. Donleavy," said Aki, pleased. "You have given us a new life and have gone beyond anything we could ever have dreamed of. It is my pleasure to assist you."

"Thank you for those kind words," Walter said. He got up, they bowed to each other and Walter left.

Aki walked Walter to the door. He stood there in the doorway, and could feel Walter's pain as he watched him get into his golf cart and slowly drive back to his own home late that night.

❖   ❖   ❖

Walter had brought Aki Watanabe over from Japan in 1975. He'd met him at a trade fair when he was looking to purchase more live Kobe beef cattle for his own two restaurants. He invited him to lunch to discuss his plans and make him an offer. Aki was surprised, and curious at the same time, but listened.

They sat down for lunch at the Yamasaki Restaurant, in Kyoto, Japan.

Walter said, "I currently have about fifty head of Kobe cattle. Many of my patrons revere my Kobe beef dinners. I currently serve it at my two restaurants, and it has always been a big hit. In addition, I want to increase my herd size to make sure I can continue to support my two restaurants. I may want to open another one or two restaurants on the East Coast later. Your compensation will be very good, and you can bring your family with you. You will have your own house and can come and go as you please."

"That is a very generous, Mr. Donleavy," Aki said, stunned.

Aki was surprised with such an extreme offer from a man he had just met. This actually came at an opportune time in Aki's life, since his parents had both passed away, his wife was an orphan, and they didn't have any brothers nor sisters.

❖   ❖   ❖

Aki also had a Master's degree in business and political science. He had trained and learned from the *masters* in martial arts, and was always on his guard. But he had a feeling that this was going to work out very well.

❖   ❖   ❖

His previous job in his younger days, he was responsible for the life of a very powerful real estate developer in Kyoto, Japan. His father and his father before him were all ninja and samurai warriors, with only one goal in life, and that was to protect. He had trained in all the martial art techniques. He went on to learn all of the secrets of the ninja assassin. He used his deadly skills only on rare occasions, but was ready if necessary.

His master had passed away, and after some time, the family didn't see a need for his services, so he was no longer obligated to serve the family anymore. His previous master also had a small Kobe beef ranch outside of Kyoto, and he began to appreciate how they raised them. He quickly found that he liked ranching. He now had a new *master* to protect who had similar ideas. He liked that.

❖ ❖ ❖

Aki smiled and asked, "Would you mind if my wife and I first come to your ranch in Rhode Island and see the surrounding area firsthand, and also what's expected of me?"

"That would be just fine." Walter smiled and said, "If you'd like, I have my own private jet that will fly us back in two days. You and your wife are welcome to join me. But once you're there, if you feel that you'd rather pass, I'll be happy to fly you and your wife back first class whenever you like."

Walter felt confident he would come and manage his ranch. He had found out from a close friend, who had been a military advisor in Japan, what Aki's previous occupation was. He was a very elite bodyguard. Many in the martial arts circuit knew and highly respected Aki. Walter also knew he could be a valuable benefit if the time ever came to use him in that capacity.

❖ ❖ ❖

Aki called Walter at the Crowne Plaza Hotel the next day and said, "My wife and I would be honored to fly with you to your home."

"That's wonderful, Mr. Watanabe," said Walter. "Why don't we meet in my hotel lobby tomorrow morning at 9:00 a.m. and go from there."

The next day the three of them took off for Rhode Island. After they were in the air for a while, Aki got up, and asked to speak with him, as he sat across from Walter.

"Why of course," Walter said pleased. "What can I do for you?"

"I'm most appreciative of the offer you made us," Aki shyly said, "It's a lot more than we dreamed of."

Walter leaned forward and said, "Aki, I'm not hiring you only to manage my cattle. I want you to be a long-term partner. I realized long ago that a paycheck is not what drives good men. In order to achieve bigger things, you have to give them an opportunity to grow. You and I will do great things together."

"Money is not necessarily a motivator for me," said Aki.

"I realized that when I first met you," said Walter. "In order for me to be successful, I need someone who is the best. Now, you may say there are others that are better than you are. I would have to disagree – because I have the best sitting in front of me right now. I just have one basic rule. I always want to know the truth. Whether it's good, or bad news, I still want to know. If it's bad, let me know as soon as possible so we can fix the problem. Please do not be afraid to make mistakes. We all make them, but many people make the bigger mistake of not learning from them."

Chapter

63

They all met at Monarch Ranch, because Walter wanted to have a special meeting with his *family*. Prior to this, Walter had a separate meeting with just Liz and Rick.

"You've spent three days listening to how Leonard restructured my companies. What you don't know is that Leonard has been taking money from the company. I found out that he had a special account in Switzerland."

"Are you kidding me?" Rick said, shocked that Leonard would do that. "How much money are we talking about?"

"About a hundred million dollars," Walter said. "Not to worry though. It's now sitting in a bank in Monaco. Fred helped me do that."

"I just can't believe it," Liz said, shocked. "After all you've been through with him over the years."

"Yes, I'm afraid so," Walter said with a sad look on his face. "In any event, we are still going forward with our plans to split up my corporation. Nothing has changed as far as I'm concerned. Now you know everything. Your guests will be arriving in the morning and I will share some of this with them. Other than that, I would like to spend a few day here and rest. There is something about this clean mountain air that is refreshing."

"You know that you can come and stay as long as you like," Rick said.

"I know, and I thank you for that," Walter said. "Now, let's see what Dianna has created for dinner."

❖ ❖ ❖

That night when everybody was at the ranch, Dianna created one of her special dishes. She made one of her specialty Vienna Schnitzel, with red cabbage soaked in white wine vinegar and potatoes au gratin with parsley. They all ate as if they hadn't eaten in a week.

"Now we know why you don't invite us up to your ranch very often," said Steve. "You don't want to share Dianna with us."

"There is no truth to that rumor," Rick said grinning. "You know you're always welcome, you just are not allowed to make her any offers to cook for you."

They all laughed and toasted to Dianna.

Dianna was standing in the kitchen, listening to the conversation and was filled with joy that everyone was satisfied with the meal.

❖ ❖ ❖

The next day after everyone arrived, and were settled, they all met in a special area outside. Walter told them certain things, including how he had divided his Monarch Enterprise Companies.

"Now you all know everything I know," said Walter.

"Thank you Walter for putting your trust in me and Liz," Rick said. "Who would have thought that I started out my life's journey being a teacher and now I'm running a cattle ranch?"

They all cheered, because each of the individuals who had been loyal to both Walter, Liz and Rick had been rewarded handsomely for their efforts. As Walter looked around the table, he felt proud to have raised *children* like his.

Walter had a business motto that he relayed to his friends and business associates *never give the person a reason to go and look for another job or leave the company, unless you want them to leave.*

"I may fly out here more often and take advantage of this clean air," Walter said taking a big breath.

Duncan also sat at the table and had to admire Walter and his accomplishments.

Chapter

64

A week later Walter said to Duncan, "Tomorrow, I want you to fly us to the Alpina-Gstaad Airport at Saanon, which is close to Bern, Switzerland," Walter spoke solemnly. "I have to visit Leonard Schultz in Gstaad. I don't want anybody to know where we are going. As far as Hilda is concerned, we are going to Munich, Germany. I'll book us into the Gstaad Palace Hotel for two nights."

"All right, I'll take care of the flight plans," said Duncan, feeling something was wrong. "Is everything all right, Mr. Donleavy?"

"Yes its fine," Walter answered glumly. "By the way Duncan. Do you remember that girl you asked me to track down? The one that said she shipped out for a tour in the military?"

"Yes I do," Duncan, said excited by the news. "Did you find out where she is stationed?"

"Yes I did," Walter said. "But you may not like it. She's actually *not* in the military as she told you she was. She lives in St

Louis, has three children and married to a Captain that *is* in the US Army. Her husband is actually in the service and deployed overseas."

"You're kidding me!" said a shocked Duncan. "But Mr. Donleavy, she sounded so sincere."

"I'm sorry Duncan, but it is what it is," Walter said

❖   ❖   ❖

They flew into the Alpina-Gstaad airport late the next night. It was raining heavily, which created a fog-like curtain, making it difficult to see through. Walter sat in the co-pilot's seat off and on the whole time since they took off from the T. F. Green Airport in Warwick, Rhode Island.

"Mr. Donleavy, you haven't said a word since we took off," Duncan said. "Is there anything I can do?"

"No you can't, Duncan," Walter responded. "I have to do this alone."

Duncan was now concerned that Walter was hiding something.

Occasionally Walter would go back to his regular seat and have his favorite tea and sugar cookies. He sat there, contemplating what he was going to say and do when he saw Leonard. He brought with him a bottle of his favorite cognac. He was going to offer it to Leonard as a last goodwill gesture.

❖   ❖   ❖

They landed and got off the plane, went through customs and walked to their rental car.

"When we get to Leonard's house, Duncan, I want you to stay in the car," Walter said looking at him, "I shouldn't be more than about twenty minutes."

"All right Mr. Donleavy," he said, not keen on leaving him alone.

It was now 9:00 o'clock at night and the rain turned into a lighter drizzle. Where Leonard lived, the air was clean and fresh. Walter had always admired his home, sitting on top of a hill like a medieval castle. His house was on the end of a long winding street. In the daytime, as you got out of the car and looked to your left and right, you could see snowcapped peaks almost all-year around. Walter walked up the steps and rang the front door bell. A few minutes later, a head peeked out through the narrow lace curtain to see who was there.

The door opened and the hinges creaked, as Leonard stood in the doorway saying tensely, "Isn't it a little late for visiting, Walter? I thought we said our goodbyes at your home?"

"Yes, it is late, and I apologize," Walter said. "But I was in the neighborhood visiting an old friend and he gave me a bottle of very old cognac. Something about one of the last batches made, before they discontinued the practice. May I come in?"

Leonard hesitated, but then said, "Of course….come in."

As Walter walked through the front door and into the living room, he marveled at what he saw.

"Would you like some tea?"

"Only if you're having some," Walter answered.

A few minutes later, Leonard brought over the tea service with two cups. Leonard poured the tea, added two sugar cubes and handed it to Walter.

"Thank you Leonard," Walter said. "Do you by any chance have any of those sugar cookies we liked so much?"

"Yes I think I do," Leonard said in a shielded way, as he went into the kitchen and brought back a small plate full.

"I would also like to leave this bottle of cognac for you," Walter said. "A final gesture of our friendship."

Walter noticed that Leonard was dressed rather sloppily, which was unlike his normal attire. His shirt looked like he'd slept in it for several days and he hadn't shaved in probably the same length of time.

Each had one cookie and Walter put down his cup after both had a few sips and said loudly, "Why Leonard! Why would you do this to me?"

"I don't know what you mean?" Leonard replied casually.

"I think you know exactly what I mean!" Walter said aloud. "I reviewed all the documents you created for myself, Rick and Liz. In very small print and in *lawyer language*, you set yourself up as the executor of not only mine, but also of Liz and Rick's estate as well. We never talked about that part."

"All right! You want to know why?" Leonard got up and shouted. "I'll tell you why! My son and wife died because of you!"

"But Leonard, your son did this to himself!" Walter shouted back. "Don't you remember the problems it caused me with all of those other investors? If it were not for me, Victor Chen would have killed Peter in a most gruesome way. I spent millions buying his freedom, even though Peter almost ruined me. All so he could play the role of a millionaire entrepreneur."

"It could have been handled differently," Leonard said, trying to stay calm.

"I have also pieced it together," Walter, said, "That *you* were the one, who put out a contract, to have me killed!"

"Yes I did!" Leonard said proudly.

"Well…for what it's worth," Walter said, "Ulrich may not be calling you anymore."

"What?" Leonard shrieked.

"And also, the people he hired, will also not be calling Ulrich anymore," Walter said.

"I don't care…I still can't forgive you!" Leonard said, now standing up, with arms flailing, which was a signal for Walter to leave.

"I'm sorry it came to this, Leonard," Walter said quietly. "I thought we had gotten past this years ago – but I guess not. In addition, don't worry, I've already un-done all the documents you created. Good-bye Leonard," he said as Walter stood up, ready to leave. "We will obviously never see each other again – this time however, for good."

Walter walked to the front door and let himself out. He walked down the steps and into the back seat of the car, which Duncan had running.

❖ ❖ ❖

Leonard stood in the doorway and watched Walter get into his car. All the while cursing to himself that he had failed to kill Walter. *Nevertheless, I'm not finished with you yet Walter,* he thought. *There is always the next day.* As they drove off, he stepped back inside his home and slammed the door shut.

❖ ❖ ❖

"Let's go, Duncan," Walter said somberly. "Let's go to the hotel, have a late snack and get a good night's sleep. We have a long flight home."

"Okay, we're on our way," Duncan said. He saw that Walter was sad, but decided not to ask him. He figured if Walter wanted him to know what happened – he'd tell him.

Walter had a restless night and finally sat up, was dressed, and waited for Duncan to take them home.

❖ ❖ ❖

The next morning Duncan and Leonard took off for home. Daylight was just peeking over the snowcapped mountaintops as they taxied down the runway, picked up speed and climbed to thirty-five thousand feet. Within minutes, they were above the clouds. Walter sat back in his favorite chair by the window. He didn't realize it, but a tear started to form in his right eye, as he thought back at all the deals he and Leonard had made together over the past forty some-odd years. He recalled how many times they had flown together in this very same plane. It was always an adventure for Walter. He had the adrenalin rush that would not stop until he succeeded with his objective.

EPILOGUE

The next day Walter went down to his cellar, where he had some of his famous paintings hanging on the wall. He went to a large flat drawer and pulled out his *partial* copy of the papyrus documents that were created in 14 BC. He looked at them one last time and closed the drawer. He still could not get over that the Egyptian Government was not interested in the long lost papyrus scrolls. However, he knew that his friend did not die in vain.

He knew that the Minister of Cultural Affairs in Cairo took the original papyrus scrolls depicting the location of the lost pyramid, and destroyed them. The current King did not want anyone to find the lost pyramid, until he had passed on.

❖ ❖ ❖

Two days later, Walter was watching an international news program when it was reported that Leonard Schultz, a longtime resident of Gstaad, Switzerland, died in his sleep. He was buried in the family crypt with his wife, Cynthia and his only son, Peter.

He turned the television off and went to bed that night, heartbroken about his friend Leonard.

❖　❖　❖

"What is the big problem here?" Rick argued. "A lot of the big ranches have their own private airfield!"

"You must understand that, while we encourage ranchers to have their own private airstrip, especially as big a ranch as yours," The Commissioner said, "We have to be cautious with how many flights will take off and land…well, you read the criteria."

They finally got their permits, and work started almost immediately. The new airstrip was being built on the Monarch Ranch after many weeks of haggling with the commissioner.

❖　❖　❖

Diana's children flew in to the Palm Springs International Airport. As they got off the airplane, they were met with tears running down their faces.

"Oh, I'm so happy you decided on Palm Desert," Diana said. "You will be very happy here."

"I'm sure we will Mother," said her daughter, Margot.

"That goes double for me," said her son, Fredrick.

"What is so great about this area is that we are very close to the Indian Wells Country Club," Diana said. "Later in the year, they have golf tournaments going on all the time, and live entertainment."

❖   ❖   ❖

Hilda and Jacob finally got married. The wedding was held in the backyard of the Monarch Ranch.

"Thank you so much for hosting our wedding," Jacob said, holding on to Hilda tightly.

"It was the least we could do for my father, and my new mother-in-law," said Rick proudly.

"That goes double for me, Mother," Liz said ecstatically.

"We both hope you'll both spend more time with us at the ranch," Rick said.

"Maybe when we come back from our vacation in Hawaii," Jacob said. "Mr. Donleavy made us reservations there."

"That's fantastic!" Liz exclaimed.

"Walter also told me that he's having Duncan fly you over there in his plane," Rick said. "While he stays here for some much needed rest from the business world."

"So please, relax and enjoy yourselves," Liz said. "And we'll see you here when you get back."

❖   ❖   ❖

Captain Owen Perkins realized that if he didn't do something about General Flannigan, then everything he'd worked for as a soldier would have been wasted. He made an appointment to go see the Judge Advocate General. On his way to see him, he thought about what this would do to his career. After thinking and re-thinking about it, he felt it was still the right thing to do, but that didn't make it that much easier.

❖   ❖   ❖

They started building a twenty-thousand square foot barn-like structure on the corner of the property of The Three Forks Restaurant and Lodge in Coeur de' Alene. As it was being built, Francisco was standing about a hundred feet away, watching them pour the foundation for the new building. They called it simply, *The Palace Entertainment Center.*

CHARACTERS – THE BERLIN ESCAPE

1. **Dr. Rick Benedict (In 1992 Rick is 42 years old)**
    a. born Jan 29, 1950 changed his name from Richard Teaubel
    b. Llama and alpaca ranches – San Lorenzo Ranch in Carrizozo, New Mexico and the St. Augustine Ranch in San Ignacio, Bolivia.
    c. Monarch Ranch Meat processing plants in Billings, Montana and Fort Collins, Colorado
2. **Dr. Elizabeth (Liz) Hildebrand. (In 1992 Liz is 41 years old)**
    a. born Mar 15, 1951 changed her name from Elizabeth Bowan
    b. Rick and Liz got married on June 11, 1987 changed name to Benedict
3. **Jennifer Billingsly** – Liz's new CFO located in Fort Collins to take care of her new companies.
4. **Liz's restaurants**
    a. The Wagon Wheel Restaurant in Fort Collins
        i. Restaurant Locations for Three Forks Restaurant and Lodge in Montana, Idaho and North Dakota

5. Walter Donleavy/Alfred Berger (<u>in 1992 Walter is 67</u>)
   a. Uncle to Rick, entrepreneur, major businessperson, has deep secrets.
   b. Born in February 27, 1925 in London England
   c. No info about Walter/Alfred before 1954
   d. Walter's two restaurants
      i. The Matterhorn – located in Manhattan, New York
      ii. The Alpinhoff – located in Providence, Rhode Island
6. Leonard Schultz – Chief lawyer and business negotiator for Walter Donleavy. Graduated from Yale in 1960. His wife's name is Cynthia. Was also the COO of Walter's business holdings.
7. Peter Schultz – Leonard's' son who started working with his father after graduating from the USC Marshall School of Business and the Leventhal School of Accounting.
8. Cynthia is Leonard Schultz wife, who died in Gstaad, Switzerland in a sanitarium.
9. Stephen Weisen – Started his own security firm called Weisen Security. He was also the captain of Liz's yacht.
   a. Created the Weisen Security Company for the US and Romanesque Security Company for all of Europe, Asia and Africa.
10. James Kingston – Vice President Special security to assist Steve with any problems. Manages the Rome operations for Weisen Security.
11. Pete Lindquist – works for Steve as part of new Weisen Security

12. Thomas Harrington - works for Steve as part of new Weisen Security, followed Roberta and Lisa from Billings, Montana to the Monarch Ranch in Colorado.

13. Duncan Houston - Walter's new pilot and Security detail. His given name was actually Hakarson, but the family changed it because it too difficult to pronounce

14. Jacob Teaubel/Fredrick & Geraldine Leiter – Gate keeper at Walter Donleavy estate (Rick's actual parent) Came over to the Unites States in 1960

15. Hilda Lowenstein/Anna & Christopher Bowens – Housekeeper at Walter Donleavy estate (Liz's actual parent) Came over to the Unites States in 1959

16. Fred Tremane – was Master Sergeant in the Army and became Forensic accountant.

17. Evan Singleton – new hires and works for Fred as a new associate.

18. Martha Honeycutt – new hires and works for Fred as a new associate.

19. Don Smith – Rick's ranch Forman at the Monarch Ranch. Maureen Smith – Don's wife

20. Danielle Smith - part time girl friend of Fred Tremane and brother of Don Smith.

21. Diana Kreutz – chef and housekeeper for Rick's Monarch Ranch main house in Fort Collins, Colorado. Was originally born in Croatia.

22. Ernie Slater – A CIA friend who taught Rick some simple burglary techniques.

23. Travis lives on the "outskirts" of the information world and knows anything that goes on the US Government.

24. Wilber Watkins – works in Ernie' office.
25. Aki Watanabe and his wife Tomichi – beef wrangler of Walter's Kobe beef ranch in Rhode Island. In his prior life was a professional Samurai bodyguard for one of the oldest and wealthiest families in Hong Kong.
26. Frank Richter – Rick's CFO for the Monarch Ranch, two meatpacking plants in Fort Collins, Colorado and Billings, Montana and the two alpaca and llama ranches. Also the son of Paul Mathews, the famous European cat burglar. He went to Yale to receive his degree.
27. Paul Mathews – Master cat burglar in Europe. Also, is the father of Frank Richter, current CFO of Monarch Enterprises.
28. Jacques Béarnaise – (was Reginald Sparling) Was the General Manager of The Alpinhoff Restaurant in Providence, Rhode Island and the Matterhorn in Manhattan. Walter gave him money and he started his own restaurant in New York called *Jacques Bistro*.
29. Milton de La Cross – Now the head chef and General Manager at The Alpinhoff Restaurant in Providence, Rhode Island.
30. Leticia Wadsworth – new back up for Milton at The Alpinhoff Restaurant.
31. Jeremy Willingham - maître de and General Manager of the Matterhorn restaurant in Manhattan. After Jacques left to start his own place, Walter divided the responsibilities of the two restaurant.
32. Dwight Robinson/Boris Bajonka – The new Master butcher for Monarch Ranch. Was originally born in Croatia and lived on the family farm until war broke out.

33. Jimmy Hackensack – an Army friend of Steve Weisen and lives in Sausalito, California. He was a tunnel rat in Vietnam. Owns a restaurant called the Seafood Peddler.

34. Dorothy Waylon – sister of Jimmy Hackensack and girlfriend of Steve

35. Victor Chen is Head of the Li Chan Group. He and Walter have made various deals together. His casinos
    a. Macau, China
        i. The Washington Resort and Casino in China
        ii. The Red Dragon Casino and Resort in Macau
        iii. The Blue Grotto Casino and Resort in Macau
    b. Johannesburg, South Africa –
        i. The Golden Reef Casino and Resort.

36. Quan Chen – Victor Chen' older son. Went to school at USC

37. General Howard Metcaff – Was the General that helped Walter get all the latest electronic equipment installed in his library and a Close friend of Walter Donleavy.

38. General Sean Flannigan – was the general who conspired with General Metcalf to find the Pyramid and the gold crown.

39. Rocky Cappellini – the loan shark who wants to be a partner in Jimmy Hackensack's restaurant The Seafood Peddler. The man Jimmy borrowed money from to help with the restaurant when he was struggling.

40. Chief Running Buffalo/Joseph Elkhorn – head Chief of all the Crow Nation in Montana. Bighorn Building – name of his corporate office.
    a. The Red Tomahawk Casino and Hotel – the first Indian Casino in Billings, Montana

    b. The White Buffalo Casino and Hotel – the other new casino in Butte, Montana

41. .Francisco Romano – manager of the Coeur D' Alene and Clearwater, Idaho, Three Forks restaurant & Lodge

42. Laura Romano – wife of Francisco and event planner for Francisco.

43. Sir Hillary von Peterborough – a famous Egyptologist who originally discovered the small pyramid of Nephritides in 1934.

44. Dr. Benjamin Fazihd – the head curator of a small Egyptian Museum named The Cairo Museum. He was also the head curator of the world famous Sir William Sheffield Museum in London, England.

45. Akar Sekhmet, the Minister of Cultural Affairs and all Archeological findings for Egypt.

46. Thomas Benjamin – met with Dr. Fazihd when he woke up at the hospital after a heart attack.

47. Dr. Albert Livingsworth – head curator of Sir William Sheffield Museum in London, who fired Dr. Benjamin Fazihd

48. General Jürgen Fieldmeister – A German Nazi Army General in 1942. Was in the Afrika Corps that was patrolling northern Africa during World War II.

49. Janus Parn – he was one of the photoengravers Walter became friends with while he was at Sachsenhausen Concentration camp.

50. Mariana Parn – wife of Janus Parn.

51. Bernhard Krueger – changed his name after the war and became a high-level banker at Reichsdeutche bank located

in Bavaria. Matthias Theisson was his name when he was in the Nazi Army and working at Sachsenhausen

52. Ulrich Pasternoff – He was a Major in the Nazi Army in charge of one of the concentration camps. He later rose to prominence in one of the largest electronic companies in Germany. He was a close friend of Bernhard Krueger.

53. Apollinaris Bonnaire (Apollo) – Has an assassin team of women living in Paris.

    a. Nansie – were on the plane watching Rick, Liz and Frank on their way to Billings.

    b. Belinda – were on the plane watching Rick, Liz and Frank on their way to Billings.

    c. Patrice – were arrested in Providence as they were waiting outside The Alpinhoff Restaurant.

    d. Alana – were arrested in Providence as they were waiting outside The Alpinhoff Restaurant. Walter drugged her to get a confession

    e. Bella Moreau – was killed by Walter while at the Creighton Hotel in London, England

    f. Sophia Mediate – tried to kill Walter while at the Kensington Palace Hotel in London, England

    g. Hellena – personal driver and assassin for Ulrich Pasternoff. She killed Bernhard Krueger as she picked him up from train station. She later killed his wife and children.

    h. Aurelia – Apollinaris private secretary and bodyguard.

    i. Roberta – assassin who tried to kill Liz and Rick at the ranch.

j. Lisa – assassin who tried to kill Liz and Rick at the ranch.

k. Taniya – Apollos' new assistant and bodyguard

54. Andre Marquise – One of Apollo's first husbands.

The next exciting adventure is called,

THE NEW YORK MACHINATIONS

Stay tuned for another thrilling episode in the lives of Liz, Rick, and Walter.

Books published and in process:

10. THE NEW YORK MACHINATIONS
(DECEMBER 2017)

9. THE BERLIN ESCAPE

8. THE ITALIAN ILLUSION

7. THE MONTANA MONOPOLY

6. THE AUSTRALIAN CONCLAVE

5. THE MOSCOW INTRIGUE

4. THE AMSTERDAM PROTOCOL

3. THE NEW MEXICO CONNECTION

2. THE COLORADO CONSPIRACY

1. THE PRAGUE DECEPTION

Go to www.NovelsByVic.com to read a brief overview about each of my books.

BIOGRAPHY - Vic Swatsek

Victor Swatsek is the author of **The Prague Deception**, **The Colorado Conspiracy**, **The New Mexico Connection**, **The Amsterdam Protocol**, **The Moscow Intrigue**, **The Australian Conclave**, **The Montana Monopoly,** and **The Italian Illusion.** **The Berlin Escape** is the ninth in a series of published novels, which follow several primary characters into thrilling adventures throughout the world. All of his books are written as a series. The first book is **THE PRAGUE DECEPTION**, and the latest book is **THE BERLIN ESCAPE**. Six to eight of the same characters are in each of his books. They don't have to be read in that order, because each book still stands on its own. However, the first book goes into more detail on the main characters.

"I want to take you on a thrilling journey with action and adventure, romance, mystery, Intrigue, and a little history thrown

in for good measure. You'll be astounded where my stories will take you."

❖ ❖ ❖

Victor is a member of the Palm Springs Writers Guild in Southern California. He has had several successful book signings.

Victor was born in Austria, and when he was seven years old, the family immigrated to the U.S. He did a tour of duty for the U.S. Army in Virginia, Texas, and Europe, and used this experience in some of his stories.

As the Senior Vice President of Production Operations for a major aerospace company, Vic managed over a thousand employees to produce a product used around the world for the airlines and heavy trucking industry.

He is the first to agree that writing a novel has many additional, interesting, and very challenging facets. His prior business experience has helped him to organize and effectively present very imaginative ideas. He grew up and still lives in Southern California with his wife, Liz.

❖ ❖ ❖

Many of my FB friends have let me know that they like the fact that my stories are global and not just in one country or city. For those of you that have not gone to my website to see what part of the world all my books will take you. (Recommend using Mozilla

Firefox) Go to my website, **www.NovelsByVic.com** "Click" on BOOKS, then scroll down to any of my books and it will take you to a flat pattern of the world. There are "pin points' which identify the country/state where a part of my story is told.